davefromqueens

Michelle Weintraub Riklan
and
Karen Weintraub

DEDICATION

In memory of our brother, David Hamilton Weintraub. We miss you.

CONTENTS

ACKNOWLEDGMENTS

This book is a legacy story to David's struggles throughout life. He overcame many obstacles, but could never fully dodge being targeted by others for being himself. His passion to make a difference in the world was marred by his awkwardness. Those who knew David well, saw a person of conviction, unbridled fervor for justice, and an unmatched kindness. He remained constant in his fight against injustice; never wavering from the pursuit of what was right. This was just one of the many lessons he passed along to his students, his friends, family, the blogging community who followed davefromqueens, and anyone else who was lucky enough to know him. While he passed away at the young age of 37 before seeing his story's conclusion, the lessons he imparted on all live on.

We would like to thank all of you who encouraged and helped us to complete this project. It's a labor of love from our hearts, a method to tell and immortalize our brother's story, and celebrate his life. Thank you to Aneta, Jolanta, Barb, Alex, Dan, Uncle Jeff, Dad and to Rob for your invaluable insights.

CHAPTER 1

David was convinced he could get this job.

When he saw close to a hundred other applicants arriving that morning at the New York City Board of Education job fair, he was surprised, but he still felt confident. He had heard the city was desperate and would hire any licensed teacher willing to brave its failing inner city schools. Even him.

A steady stream of young men and women dressed in new, but inexpensive suits and dresses were parading into the school gymnasium. It seemed the size of an aircraft hangar to David and it had been set up with row after row of gray metal folding chairs, all facing a makeshift podium, and at the back of the cavernous room were eight card tables, each with two chairs kitty-cornered, set up for preliminary interviews.

David was ready.

He took a seat in the front row and shortly a young, heavyset black woman sat down next to him. She kept dabbing at the perspiration on her cheeks and forehead with a large white hanky and David could feel the warmth from her large body. He was over two hundred and eighty pounds himself, but he hadn't felt warm until the woman sat down next to him. He began playing with the shirt button just above his beltline and hoped she wouldn't talk to him.

He wouldn't be sitting there at all, he thought, if his voice wasn't so high and squeaky. He had wanted to be a radio sports announcer and had gotten his Bachelor's degree three years earlier at Ithaca College in TV and radio communications. He knew every stat from every football, basketball, baseball and hockey game and every tennis and golf match ever played, but his voice was too high-pitched for radio, he was told, and when he started speaking, he could never stop himself from going on and on, faster and faster, spitting out all the facts he had collected in his mind over the years.

No one would hire him. He hadn't even lasted as a volunteer

covering some of the local high school games, and he'd often overheard one of the other Port Jefferson High School announcers making fun of him.

He spent a year trying to come to grips with the loss of his dream to be an announcer and with the death of his mother from lung cancer the previous summer. He still lived at home then and he would rent movies and watch them, one after another, all day long. One day he rented *Dead Poets Society*. To him, it showed everything that was right and everything that was wrong about the world. He was mesmerized by it. He watched it over and over for three days straight until he became certain he would be a good teacher.

The next morning he brought it back, paid the late fines, and drove over to Long Island University where he enrolled to start his Master's in education the following semester.

He had always loved kids anyway.

"Why don'tcha turn on the air conditioning in here?" the woman next to him yelled out to a man in a nicely pressed tan suit who had walked over to check the microphone at the podium in front of them.

"If you don't like it, you can leave," he called back to her.

She stood up and walked out.

David couldn't make out the words she was mumbling under her breath as she stormed out. He liked her for not putting up with the rudeness of the man in the tan suit, but he became embarrassed for her. Everyone sitting in the chairs behind him had gone silent as they watched her walking defiantly back to the entry doors of the gymnasium.

She let the double doors slam behind her and after a minute, the hubbub of chatter resumed behind David, but not as loudly as before.

Finally a middle-aged woman in a loose floral dress came to the podium, tapped the mike once, and began to speak. She told the audience that there were positions open for licensed teachers, but only in those city schools marked as under "registration review."

Okay, the worst ones, David thought. The ones whose students were most in need of competent teachers. The ones who needed Robin Williams. The ones who needed me.

As the woman at the podium went on in her resonant voice about what teachers could expect in those schools that were hiring, more and more applicants stood up, individually and in pairs, and walked back out through the entry doors.

David knew he was in.

By the time the woman pointed to the interview tables behind her, which now had a Board of Education employee at each, there were about twenty applicants left sitting. David stood and made his way over to the closest interview table. Behind him, a dozen others did the same.

David sat down with a thin balding man in rolled up shirtsleeves who took all David's paperwork and started going through it. He paused to stare at David every few seconds. David's eyes wandered back and forth. He knew he had brought the exact paperwork and all the credentials he needed. Why did this bald man keep looking up at him?

"I'm not sure, Mr. Weintraub, that we have a position open for you that will make you happy," the man said and started to slide the sheaf of paperwork back across the little table toward David.

"I don't want to be happy. I want to be employed," David said. He leaned forward and stretched his large frame across the table to peer down at the list of openings on the piece of mimeographed paper in front of the man.

"Let's see what you've got here," David said to him and smiled at the man with as much innocence as he could muster.

The man also hunched over the list and ran his finger down the column of openings.

"Well, there is one fifth grade spot in Brooklyn we might consider. Bushwick. PS 232."

"232?" David said. "A perfect palindrome. I'll take it." He gave the man another broad, expectant smile.

"Well, alright. I guess that might work." The man took a blank form and slid it across the table for David to start filling out with the blue Bic pen he handed him. As David filled in box after box on the standard hiring form, the bald headed man kept staring at him as if there was something he still wasn't quite sure about.

David was back out the entrance doors in less than twenty minutes after he had first sat down at the table.

He was a teacher.

"These are your children."

Charles L. Schneider, Vice Principal of PS 232 in Brooklyn, held the heavy metal door open so David could peer into the room. The twenty-three fifth graders ignored the two men in the doorway and carried on doing what they'd been doing. The boys stood together in twos and threes and elbowed each other roughly and laughed. The girls giggled with each other in little groups or taught each other new dance moves at the back of the room. Not one child sat at a desk.

"Hate to throw a big guy like you to these wolves, but here you go," Schneider said. "First day of school's always rough." He wrinkled his nose and pushed his face up into the air for a second as he walked into the classroom, leaving David to catch the heavy red door as it slammed against his shoulder.

"Alright!" Vice Principal Schneider yelled. "Into your seats. All of you."

David heard the boys peppering each other with comments, all in Spanish, as they chose seats in the back of the room. The girls were left with the first two rows of desks to sit in.

"You're in the fifth grade now," Schneider said after the last boy, who seemed older than the rest, had taken his seat at the back corner desk. The other boys had apparently agreed to save that spot for him because it was the least conspicuous. David wondered who he was. He looked big. Maybe he'd stayed back a year. Or two.

"This is your teacher for this year. Mr. Weintraub," Schneider said.

"David?" Schneider lowered his voice to speak his name and he turned and beckoned David with his finger to come into the classroom from the doorway where he'd been standing. David felt like a student himself and he realized Schneider hadn't smiled once since he'd first met him in his office early that morning.

David's arms remained motionless at his sides and his palms splayed out at right angles as he took four long steps across the linoleum floor to stand next to Schneider. At six foot four, David was almost half a foot taller than the Vice Principal. As David stood there, he could see some of the little faces squinting up at him, trying to make out just what kind of jerk this new teacher would be.

David stared at his students. Everything he had prepared the night before to say to them, whoever they were, was now deeply buried under the anxious confusion that had taken over his mind when the Vice Principal had introduced him. One, two, three, four, five, six, seven, he counted. One, two, three, four, five, six, seven.

Schneider folded his arms across his chest and waited for David to speak.

"Okay. Your lives are about to change," David said, stepping forward a few feet. His eyes were wandering back and forth from his nervousness, but it looked like he was scanning his students and looking at each of them, one at a time, as his eyes moved back and forth across the room. "So's mine. No one has paid much attention to PS 232. No one has paid much attention to you. Your future hasn't been important to anyone. It is important to me. That's why I'm going to teach you those three R's, readin', 'ritin', 'rithmetic. So you can have a future. So I can have a future too, really. See? We're in this together."

David felt he was on a roll now and he continued as new thoughts quickly flowed through his mind.

"Why haven't we been given any future? Because we're the little guys. Even as large as I am, I'm still one of the little guys. So are you. So are your parents. So's this little neighborhood down here in Bushwick. We're all the little guys. The big guys, the big guys are over there across the East

River. In Manhattan,in the banks, in the corporate offices, in the mayor's office. We're just the little guys over here. We don't matter to them. But if we can have a future, we can matter. If we know our three R's, we can matter. If I can teach you your three R's, you can matter. That's all I'm going to be doing here. Making you matter."

David didn't know where all that had come from, but once he'd started, hesitantly, it just began to roll on out, freely. He looked around at the faces in front of him and he could focus on each one now. None were smiling, but he could see they all were paying attention, at least, even if they didn't quite know what to make of him.

That was okay. David was used to that.

He turned around to look at Schneider, but the Vice Principal had left the room while David was talking.

A month later David could feel the October air had started to turn crisp in the morning as he waited on the Bayside, Queens subway platform for his 6:19 car into Brooklyn. He was getting to enjoy the twenty-minute ride now that he felt more comfortable with the same passengers he saw every morning. There was an easy familiarity with them now and he didn't worry about threats or embarrassments. Most of the other passengers traveled on into Manhattan to their secretarial and middle management jobs. David had never seen anyone else get off in Brooklyn, let alone in Bushwick.

PS 232 was only two blocks from his subway station, but even before seven on this cool October morning, three young Puerto Rican men were hanging together in front of the bodega David had to pass, their hands cupped together in front of their mouths as they blew warm air into their fingers. A cloud of cigarette smoke lingered in the air above them.

David reached the school and nodded to Freddie, the school security guard standing by the front doors, letting the teachers in and keeping the students out of the three story tan brick building. Freddie Donnelly had been friendly to David since his first day at school and David often chatted with him for a minute before he went upstairs to his class room. David thought he and Freddie were about the same age and they seemed to share a bond because of that, but David could see Freddie was proud of his crisply pressed uniform and the little badge on his shirt. David knew it would never be a good idea to cross him.

The school had been built in the late sixties, before Bushwick had self-destructed, and this morning David's second floor classroom felt cool to him as he entered it, as if the metal frame of the building itself had grown cold overnight.

He set down his papers, his math text, and a new pack of cards on his desk and popped open the diet Pepsi he'd brought with him. His throat pulsed with the four long swallows he took before setting the can down. By the time Miranda Gonzalez, his first student every morning, had walked in and had taken her front row seat, the can was empty and he'd hidden it under the paper trash in his basket from the day before.

When all of his students who were going to be there that day had taken their seats and the eight o'clock buzzer had sounded throughout the classrooms, David remained seated at his desk and looked around the room smugly, as if he had a secret. After a few seconds looking at them, he broke out into one of his silly faces – this one with an exaggerated smile and raised eyebrows over wide, wide open eyes – which he'd been practicing in the little cabinet mirror in his bathroom for the last several weeks.

"Okay," he said, "Everybody gather around my desk. I'm going to show you a card trick."

There was a rush of movement in front of him, feet pattering across the floor, until his class was huddled together around his large wooden desk, girls in front, boys behind peering over their shoulders or looking down between the girl's heads at the new pack of cards now by itself in the center of the desk. Jesus, the tallest boy in the class, stood behind everyone, expressionless beyond the hint of disdain he always carried on his face.

"This is a version of Three Card Monte," David said as he opened the pack and slid out the deck of blue Bicycle cards. He took the cards into his hands, did three quick Hindu shuffles, and set the deck down.

He turned it over once, pulled out the two jokers and the ace of spades, and held them up facing the class so they could look closely at the three cards.

"I am not showing you this trick so you can take a five dollar bill off the Rodriguez brothers next spring when they set up their little card table in front of Marino's deli. I'm showing you this so you can improve your powers of observation. It'll be fun. You know, if you're reading a chapter book, you need to be able to observe clearly what all the characters are doing. If you're doing a division problem, you need to observe clearly all the parts of the problem in order to solve it. Outside this classroom, the more clearly you can observe what is going on around you, the less likely you are to be taken advantage of by anything. Now, watch this. And watch it carefully."

David kept the three cards in one hand and slid the remainder of the deck over to the left side of his large desk. The smile on his face was now genuine.

"So, we've got these three cards here, two jokers and the ace of spades, right?"

He held the three cards together, face down in front of him and then he seemed to pull one card off the top and flip it over. It was a joker. He put it back. He pulled one card off the bottom, or so it seemed, and he flipped it over. It too was a joker. He pulled out and showed them the face of the middle card next, except he'd deftly pulled the two top cards off together this time, so what they saw was the ace.

"Right?" he asked again.

"Right"!" most of the class murmured.

"So. The joker's on top, right?" David asked them.

"Right!"

He flipped over the top card. It was the ace of spades.

"Whoa! How'd you do that?" they all wanted to know.

"Watch. Watch carefully," David told them. "What card is on bottom?"

"The other joker!" several girls yelled out.

He flipped the bottom card over. Now it was the ace of spades.

"Get out!" the two girls right by his desk yelled.

They looked at each other and shook their heads. All the kids behind them were whistling, smiling or shaking their heads. They knew they were being tricked, but still it was fun. Only Jesus remained without expression.

David kept shuffling the three cards and asking them to identify which card was on the top, on the bottom or in the middle. They guessed wrong every time, but before they became frustrated, David knew enough to stop.

He finally held out the joker, the ace of spades and the second joker so they could see them all and then he lay all three cards face down on the desk next to each other.

"What's this one?" he asked and put his finger on the card to his left.

"A joker," everyone yelled.

David turned it over. It was.

"And this one?" David. He pointed to the one on his right.

"The ace of spades!"

"You're right," he said and turned it over. "Now, what's this one?" and he pointed to the card in the middle.

"The other joker!" everyone but Jesus shouted.

"Oops!" David said and turned over the middle card. It was the Jack of Hearts.

No one said a word.

"Want to know how I did it?" David asked them, his face beaming.

Almost every head nodded.

"Okay," David said. "First I have to show you how to do what's called a double lift and then a top slide. Here. Watch this."

David showed them how he manipulated the cards each time he flipped them over so that they thought they were seeing the top card, but were really viewing the middle or the bottom card. He explained it carefully and then he slowly, slowly moved the cards in his hands so they could see the sleight of hand each time he repeated the maneuver.

Suddenly Jesus began shouting at him over the heads of all the students.

"You know what, man? You are effin' weird! You are just weird, doin' that here!"

David just managed to dodge the textbook that barreled at him from Jesus' right hand and smacked against the concrete wall behind David.

"Effin' weird!" Jesus repeated loudly as he walked back and sat down at his desk in the corner, his arms folded tightly across his chest, disdain on his face.

David felt himself hyperventilating. Not now, please, not now, he thought. He held onto the sides of his wooden chair with thick, moist hands. One, two, three, four, five, six, seven. One, two, three, four, five, six, seven.

"Jesus, you crazy!" one of the girls yelled back to the corner of the room and then turned to David. "Don't you pay 'tention to him, Mr. Weintraub."

"Yeah, he's crazy," several other girls whispered.

David took a deep breath.

"Alright then, class," he said. "Who wants to be first practicing how to do this? Miranda?"

David held out the three cards to her and she took them from his hand.

Today was hardly the first time David had been called weird, but it was not until he settled into his seat on the train for his ride home that his mind returned, beyond his control, to play through that moment with Francine Belmont one morning when he was eleven.

As soon as David had woken up that day, he remembered that Miss McCarthy was going to take his sixth grade class down to the Port Jefferson docks to watch the Bridgeport ferry come in. Yesterday she had started giving his class a history of the harbor and today they were actually going down to see it.

It was going to be a good day, David thought, a really good day.

Even if Billie or Matthew teased him today, he'd still have a good time watching the ferry, counting the people and cars on it and smelling the salt water of Long Island Sound. It was only early May, but already the water was warming and releasing its briny aroma into the air.

His parents never took him to the harbor – or anywhere, really, anymore -- because his mother was too frightened he'd create a "scene."

David rolled over on his back and stretched his arms up across his pillow and rested them on either side of his head. The spring sun was just coming through his bedroom window and the light in his room seemed quiet and soft. Safe.

Sometimes, school wasn't all that bad, he mused, lying there. He liked history and math best, history because he liked learning all the dates and finding out about everything that had already happened in the past. That way there were no surprises. That way you didn't have to worry about the future. And math. He loved math. He was so good at numbers, and numbers were so certain. You always knew exactly what each one meant, what each one was. Numbers were facts. They had no sadness, no fear in them. No anger.

One, two three, four, five, six, seven.

Sometimes when they were at recess in the playground and one of the kids had called him a name – "weirdo" or "Jew boy," usually, sometimes "bagel boy" -- he'd sit over on the cool metal bars of the jungle gym by himself and count all the bricks in the side of the school building. Miss McCarthy was nice. She'd let him do that. She knew how good he was at math.

"David! What are you doing up there? You're going to be late for the bus!"

Ut-oh. Mom.

One, two, three four, five, six, seven.

David pulled himself out of bed and, yawning loudly, walked over to his bedroom door. He opened it, peeked into the hallway and then scooted down to the bathroom in his underwear. His younger sister Karen was already downstairs. Michelle, three years older, had already left for high school.

He closed the door of the little white room and lifted the lid on the toilet seat. He tried to spell "ferry" in the water with his yellow pee, but he ran out before he reached the "y." He flushed, turned to the sink, splashed some water on his face, and picked up his toothbrush. He liked having his own little spot in the toothbrush holder – he almost felt like part of the family -- and he was happy that this time he had a blue brush. He didn't like the green ones he sometimes ended up with. Green seemed like less of a fact to him than blue.

After brushing and spitting, he ran the water hard in the sink and slid his hand carefully all around the inside of the white enamel so that there could be no trace of his spit or his toothpaste.

Can't have that. Mom wants it clean.

Back in his room, the sun had risen high enough now that it shone through his window and created a long shadow from the bedpost across the beige rug. He closed his door behind him and stepped up to the edge of the shadow so that it seemed to stretch back out all the way across his room from his groin.

He loved doing that.

His clothes were laid out on his dresser and he was just struggling to

17

pull his tee shirt over his shoulders when he heard his mom again.

"David! Hurry up!"

One, two, three, four, five six seven.

He walked down the stairs and turned down the hall to the kitchen. As he passed the living room, he looked in to see if the white shag rug had any footprints in it. Good. There weren't any. It was all still perfectly smooth from last night's vacuuming. Nobody was in trouble.

His younger sister, Karen, was just finishing her bowl of Rice Chex when he slid into his chair across the corner of the kitchen table from her. David grabbed the bowl, milk and cereal box that were already on the table and set up his breakfast spot. He placed a double thickness of paper towels on top of the white placemats under his cereal bowl. Just in case.

"Hey," Karen said as she walked her empty bowl over to the dishwasher.

David began talking immediately.

"Karen, did you know that Port Jeff was originally called Brookhaven and the original settlers bought a tract of land form the Setalcott Indians in 1655 and named it Sowassett, which means 'where the water opens,' but they never started building ships until 1797 and they didn't build the causeway until 1836 to stabilize the flooding..."

David's head moved back and forth ever so slightly, almost but not quite swaying, and his large brown eyes looked left and right from under his thick dark lashes as he continued rattling off as fast as he could all the facts and figures Miss McCarthy had given them yesterday about the history of Port Jefferson.

Karen saw how excited he was about seeing the ferry today and she figured every fact he repeated was perfectly correct -- as it always was -- but she did not want to miss the bus and be punished by mom.

"Tell me the rest outside. Hurry up."

After David had spooned the last bite of Wheaties -- Breakfast of Champions, he thought...he loved that -- into his mouth before he had run for the door, he heard the vacuum starting up out in the living room and running back and forth, back and forth, in long strokes across the thick white rug.

Standing outside, at the end of their driveway, David finished telling Karen everything he had learned in class the day before about Port Jefferson.

Karen knew he probably remembered more about it today than Miss McCarthy did. She kept nodding her head so he knew she was really listening to him.

When he had given out the last fact, David looked next door at the first of the many white, two story wooden houses that lined their street and made up their neighborhood.

"Oh, no. Where's Sean?" he asked.

"Isn't today his dentist appointment?" Karen asked.

"Oh, no," David repeated and started moving the thumb of his right hand quickly back and forth, back and forth, across the inside tips of his fingers. One, two, three, four, one, two, three, four.

Karen knew these signs.

"You can check on Sean when you get home and tell him all about your trip."

David stopped fidgeting his right hand while he paused to think about that. Then he gave his sister an exaggerated wink and a smile appeared on his face.

"Yeah, but I might not tell him *everything*," he said.

David heard the school bus accelerating up their street after it had turned the corner on to their block. His eyes were still not quite back in focus, but he eased Karen forward to the end of the driveway and put his hand around her little shoulder as they waited for the bus to pull up.

David was still thinking about Sean, who always protected David from the mean kids and consoled David when kids called him names. Sean would stick his index finger into the air in front of him to insist the other kids let David play dodgeball or kickball in the playground during recess.

David had learned to do that with Karen, too, and had demanded she be brought into the games with the neighborhood kids. She was four years younger than he was and she sometimes had no interest in playing, but she'd always join in to make David happy after she saw him championing her, thrusting his index finger in the air, too, just like Sean did.

The yellow bus pulled up in front of them, its air brakes hissing, and the tall doors unfolded so the two of them could step up.

"Today's gonna be a good day," David whispered to his sister as she stepped onto the bus.

He reached out with his left hand and grabbed the metal railing inside the doors to help pull himself up onto the first step behind Karen. The thick iron felt cool to his touch and its weight was reassuring to him. It was solid. It was a fact. It was like a number.

He raised his foot up onto one step and then another until he reached the rubber mat at the front of the bus aisle and he turned to the left and quickly grabbed onto the metal rail on top of the first seat to his left.

He looked down the length of the bus. It seemed narrower, tighter, closer to him this morning as he looked out at the thirty kids in front of him, watching him. What had they been saying to each other about him this morning, he wondered. One, two, three, four, five, six seven.

He swung his hands from one seat back to the next as he made his way down the aisle, walking fast, but awkwardly between the seats and toward the last row on the right in the far back where he always sat. Karen was already four steps in front of him, making her own way to the seat in the back of the bus.

David knew the brown Naugahyde would be cool when he sat on it, and from the left side of the bus he would be able to see the cemetery they passed every day on their way to school. He liked to see how many headstones he could count before the bus turned the corner at the end of that block. Once he got up to one hundred and thirty-eight.

Half way down the aisle Francine Belmont, a little first grader, suddenly got up out of her seat after Karen had passed her and stood directly in front of David, her hands firmly on the hips of her blue dress.

David moved his eyes to the left and to the right, looking for an escape, but there was nowhere to go. He stopped and held on tightly to the back of the seats on either side of him.

"You know what?" Francine screamed up at him. "You are weird! You're just plain weird!" and with that she pulled her right arm back and slammed him in the stomach as hard as she could with her fist.

David doubled over and dropped to the rubber mat on the floor. Francine sat back down in her seat and looked at the little girl next to her, waiting for praise for what she'd just done.

No one on the bus said anything.

Karen turned around and came back to David, reached down and helped him up. He was sobbing and shaking and his nose ran and covered his lips and chin with moisture. As she helped David down the aisle to his seat, Karen saw one boy point at David's face, elbow his seatmate, and giggle.

The bus driver watched everything in the rear view mirror, and just as Karen and David reached their seats, he slammed the bus into gear and drove off.

Karen looked across the aisle at David. He stopped sobbing, wiped his nose with his sleeve, and just stared away from her out the window.

After a minute, Karen heard him repeating something under his breath.

"It is not a good day. It is not a good day. One, two, three, four, five, six, seven."

CHAPTER 2

The morning after Jesus had thrown the book at him, David took the early train in so he could report the incident first thing to Mr. Schneider in his office.

"Mr. Weintraub, we're in Bushwick," Schneider said after hearing David's description of the event. "There are heroin overdoses, drive by shootings, gang stabbings on this very block, every night and every day. Jesus threw a book? I'm so sorry. Now, why don't you go find something more important to do than waste my time with this foolishness?"

David held himself back from telling Schneider that there were no drive by shootings or gang stabbings in his classroom and that he wanted to keep it that way by squashing any incidents like this before they got worse. These were eleven-year-old kids – except for Jesus – and it was his duty to protect them.

Instead, David only nodded and started to object, mildly, but Mr. Schneider had already walked past him and out the door of his office. David stood there by himself listening to his footsteps echoing quietly down the hallway.

David went upstairs to his own classroom, sat down at his desk, slipped the diet Pepsi out of his briefcase and drank. He'd hidden his empty can under yesterday's trash by the time Miranda arrived fifteen minutes later, and he was calm again.

"I've got these for you," he said to her as she walked to her desk. "Come look."

He slid a pastel colored notebook across his desk toward her along with a pack of six ball-tip pens, two black, the others green, red, blue, and purple. He'd gone shopping at Staples the previous Saturday and had picked up two dozen notebooks and pen packs for his class because almost none of his students' families could afford them, and the school provided his class with almost nothing but chairs, desks, chalk and erasers.

He'd spent almost two hundred dollars on the supplies, but he knew he could make up the deficit in his own budget by spending next Saturday afternoon at any poker table in Atlantic City. He loved poker. The rules were simple, and most everything else was mathematics. He'd put himself through graduate school by spending his Saturday afternoons at Bally's, the Tropicana and the Golden Nugget.

"Thank you, Mr. Weintraub," Miranda said as she gathered his gifts to her chest.

As the other students began to arrive, David handed each of them a notebook and pack of pens. A line formed by his desk while each student waited for David to pull out one notebook and one pen pack from his briefcase. He had to ease each notebook out from the briefcase on the floor next to him so he didn't bend the cardboard corners or scratch the one next to it with the coiled plastic bindings.

Every student thanked him, some loudly, some quietly.

Jesus came in just as the first period buzzer vibrated through the air of the classroom and David beckoned him over.

"These are for you, Jesus," David said. "Also, I've moved your desk up to the front row, there on the far left. I want you to sit there from now on, closer to me." He winked at Jesus. "We can be buddies."

Two of the girls in the second row giggled loud enough for both David and Jesus to hear.

Jesus looked down at his notebook and pens as if they might be another trick of some kind. He mumbled something David couldn't understand. Maybe it was in Spanish, David thought. It wasn't "thank you," though.

Jesus turned and walked over to his desk and kicked the leg of the chair once to push it back so he could sit in it. He chucked the notebook and pens onto his desk and for a second the "whap" as they hit the surface was the only sound in the classroom.

Two weeks later Jesus threw an eraser.

David had sent little Bobby Martinez to the board to write out the two division problems David was going to go over with the class. Bobby was the most conscientious boy in the class and David knew it made him happy when David chose him to put the examples up on the board.

He wrote out each number so slowly and so carefully, though, that the rest of the class would start to yell at him "Hurry up, Bobby, will ya!" but when he was done, each numeral was perfectly chalked and perfectly in line with every other number in the column.

David stood by the side of his desk, his arms straight down, his hands splayed out, fingers moving up and down, as he watched Bobby's little hand writing painstakingly on the board.

Suddenly an eraser snapped Bobby's head forward and left a rectangle of chalk dust down the back of his head and across his blue shirt collar.

David ran over to him as several of the children shouted, "Jesus did it!"

David turned Bobby to face him and placed his hands on Bobby's shoulders. Bobby's eyes were moist, but he wasn't crying.

"I wouldn't give Jesus my water yesterday in the caf when he asked me," Bobby whispered up to David. "I embarrassed him in front of his friends 'cause I wouldn't obey him."

"Are you okay?" David asked him and turned him back around to look at the back of his head.

"I'm okay," Bobby said.

"You and Miranda are in charge of the class while I'm gone. Sit at my desk." David turned to face Jesus. "You. Come with me."

David wanted to grab Jesus by his earlobe, like his mother used to do to him until it hurt, and pull him down the hallway, but he didn't dare. He knew the rules. So did Jesus.

In the hallway David walked right next to the boy, aware of how small and frail he seemed next to him even though Jesus always looked so big next to the other fifth graders. David's cordovans echoed loudly over the quiet slapping of Jesus' sneakers as they walked quickly down the empty corridor to Schneider's office.

"I want to see the Vice Principal," David said to Schneider's secretary, Mrs. McCaffrey, as he burst into the office. He was out of breath.

"He's not here today, Mr. Weintraub," the secretary said. She had a string of colored glass beads around her neck with her glasses attached to it, just like David's aunt Mildred used to wear. They always looked so funny, David thought.

"Jesus threw something again today. An eraser. He hit Bobby Martinez," David said.

"I see," she said.

"I want him put in detention."

"Only Mr. Schneider can do that."

"That's not right."

"It may not be, Mr. Weintraub.'

"He didn't do anything the first time I reported Jesus threw something."

"I know."

She paused, appraising David and then looking over at Jesus, who was still standing back by the office door.

"Mr. Weintraub, you'll have to take this...this boy, back to your classroom today, but why don't you come back here yourself at the end of the school day."

"But you said Mr. Schneider won't be here today."

"But I will," Mrs. McCaffrey said.

"Oh. Okay."

"Go ahead and lock the door behind you," Mrs. McCaffrey said when David arrived that afternoon. "Let's sit over here." She motioned to a faded brown leather sofa under the room's one window.

David felt nervous as he sat down and even more so when Mrs. McCaffrey sat down next to him. She must have been sixty years old, but she was a woman. And she'd asked him to lock the door. Was she going to break the rules?

"David...I can call you David?" She touched his hand and he gripped his knee harder.

He nodded. One, two, three, four, five, six, seven.

"You're not only new to Bushwick. You're new to teaching -- but I have heard you're good with the kids. Heard you are actually teaching them something. I don't want to see you get eaten alive here. This is between us, okay?"

David nodded again. He felt his eyes widen, but it wasn't one of the moves he'd practiced in his bathroom mirror.

Mrs. McCaffrey leaned closer to David as she talked.

"You're not going to get any support from Schneider. Let me tell you a couple things about him. Before he ever came here, he had been made a gym teacher at PS 473 because he couldn't handle a classroom. Turned out, he couldn't handle gym either. He spent most of his time at 473 drumming up false allegations against other teachers. He's one of those guys who has to tear others down, you know, just to make himself look better. I'm just being honest with you, David. They finally made him a Vice Principal there, just to keep him out of the way. Mrs. Bachelder, the Principal – I worked for her back in the sixties, a nice gal, but she burned out – sat him at a desk by one of the exits selling Snickers bars, Gumdrops and Tootsie Pops to people who came in and out. The school could raise some extra money for supplies, she said, but really, she was just keeping Schneider out of everybody else's hair. That's what the Vice Principal position in a school is for now, you know. It's for hiding bad apples. Then Schneider got caught impersonating the principal at a PTO meeting and that's when the district office shipped him over here. Mrs. Harrison, our principal -- you haven't met her yet and maybe, hopefully, never will -- made the mistake of putting him in charge of morning auditorium one day last year, and he lost control of the students. While they were jumping around and yelling, one kid – Jesus, he's the one in your class – got up on the stage and set three cardboard boxes on fire. The smoke filled the entire school and three fire trucks had to be called to get the situation under control. That's Mr. Schneider for you. You need to know that, and nobody else is going to tell you."

Mrs. McCaffrey leaned against the back of the sofa and relaxed her body as if she'd just finished a fifty-yard dash.

"Are you going to get in trouble for telling me this?" David asked her.

"Not unless you tell on me. Besides, I'm retiring this year. How much trouble could I get into?"

"I won't tell. Honest."

"I just want you to know what you're up against here. I have no idea why you wanted to come here to teach. You live out in Bayside, right? Queens."

"Yes. None of my interviews to teach on Long Island had gone very well."

"I see."

David watched her face as she went over something in her mind. He was beginning to feel pretty sure he was going to be getting into trouble for this, even if she didn't.

"David, the best advice I can give you is to just forget the book and eraser incidents. Go on doing what you're doing in the classroom. Mr. Wilson – you know, he has the classroom next to yours -- has told me you're good. You care. I can see how the kids would like you."

David fidgeted with his hands a second and then stood.

"I've still got to talk to Mr. Schneider tomorrow. This isn't right. Everybody's got to play by the rules. Even Schneider. My other kids don't feel safe around Jesus. I'm sorry, Mrs. McCaffrey."

She looked up at him. God, he was big.

"I'm sorry too, David."

She got up and opened the door for David to leave.

Forty-five minutes later David walked down between the two long wings of his three-story apartment building and entered the lobby at the end of the quadrangle. He was still agitated after his meeting with Mrs. McCaffrey and he tapped one foot and then the other and sipped from his Slurpee while he waited during the elevator's slow descent from the third floor.

He got off the elevator on the second floor and began the long walk down the wing to his right toward his apartment, the last on the right at the end of the thinly carpeted corridor, right across from Mrs. Blinkoff's.

Inside his apartment, he set his bulging briefcase down by the door, walked over and looked out through the large living room window at the traffic on 48th Street for a moment and then sat on the couch and pushed the coffee table aside so he could stretch his feet out into the middle of the small room.

David had lived here for more than two years, ever since graduate school, but the off-white walls were still bare. Besides the couch and the thin coffee table, there was only a TV and a VCR on a stand and a large, dark bookcase against the wall opposite the window. The top two shelves held books, mostly hardcover textbooks and sports anthologies, all arranged alphabetically. The next shelf down had a collection of videos, also arranged alphabetically, and the bottom two shelves held a collection of games in worn and faded boxes with the cardboard split along the edges on most of them. Clue, Monopoly, MasterMind, Sorry, Parcheesi, checkers and chessboards, Uno, decks of cards, used and unopened, all stacked neatly on top of each other in tall columns.

As a child, on rainy Saturdays, David would grab one of his father's yellow legal pads and go from room to room throughout the house taking a written inventory of all the games the family had. When he was sure he had listed them all, he would find his sister Karen and together they would go through and play every game in the house, ticking them off one by one on David's pad as they finished each. It would take all day.

His father was usually at work on weekends, or at least he was seldom home, his mother was in her room doing crossword puzzles, his older sister Michelle was off with her friends and he and Karen were left to their days of endless game playing. David loved it.

As he sat slumped now against the back cushion of the sofa, David scanned all the boxes on the bottom shelves and thought about all the rules of all the games that he still knew by heart. That's what he needed now. He needed the rules of the game he was playing at PS 232.

How can you play a game if you don't know the rules? How can you win if you don't know the rules?

He breathed slowly and deeply. Okay, so he couldn't be a sports announcer, but that wasn't his fault. It was his body's. He couldn't help it if his voice was too high and if it ran away with him when he got too excited. But it turned out he loved teaching. He was doing good for these kids. He was sure of that.

He was worried about Schneider, though. He didn't want to fight him. He could lose. He could get fired. What else in the world was there that he could do besides teach?

He didn't know.

Schneider was wrong. David was sure of that. If he didn't fight Schneider, the kids would lose. Jesus had to be put in another class or at least be forced to behave in David's so the kids could be safe. That was only fair, only right.

If he didn't protect his kids, David concluded, he would be the one who was wrong.

He pushed himself up off the sofa and went into his bedroom. He sat down at the little desk at the end of his bed where his computer was and turned it on.

After searching for a couple of minutes, he clicked on the PDF he'd been looking for. "New York City School Rules and Regulations, Discipline Code." He started reading.

Before he went to bed that night, he took the Monopoly box from the shelf and sat down on the sofa with it. He pulled off the faded cover and pushed the tokens and dice around with his index finger until he found what he was looking for. He picked up the little tin cannon and looked at it.

He'd always been the top hat. Well, maybe sometimes, the little tin car. Never the cannon. He didn't like guns. But, if you're going to war…it might help to have a good luck charm.

He set the tiny cannon down on the coffee table, put the lid back on the box, and returned his Monopoly set to the shelf.

The next morning, as he walked toward his front door to leave for school, he picked up the cannon from the table and slid it into his pants pocket.

He arrived at school early again and went straight to Schneider's office. The night before he'd read that throwing any objects at another student or a teacher in a classroom – books, erasers, water bottles, anything – was grounds for an automatic five-day suspension. He was going to demand the Vice Principal suspend Jesus.

When David pushed open the door to the office, Schneider was standing next to Mrs. McCaffrey's desk looking at some papers she'd just handed him. Schneider turned, expressionless, toward David.

"What do you want now?" Schneider asked.

"Jesus threw an eraser yesterday. He hit Bobby Martinez in the back of the head. I want you to suspend Jesus. Five days. It's in the rules."

"Send him to me later this morning," Schneider said. "I'll talk to him then. Doesn't sound like a big deal. I'm on my way to the district office now."

Papers in hand he walked past David and out the front door of the office.

David looked at Mrs. McCaffrey.

"If there's no incident," Mrs. McCaffrey said, "there doesn't have to be a report. If there's no report, there's no statistic. If there's no statistic, Bushwick looks good, because it now has fewer violent incidents.

Reported."

"I get it," David said. "Schneider's rules." Just like his mother had had her own rules, the rules that had always made her right, righter and smarter than David, it had always seemed to him.

One, two, three, four, five, six seven.

He suddenly wasn't able to focus his eyes on Mrs. McCaffrey and he kept looking back and forth across the room from the window to the wall and back to the window again.

"Yes, David. I'm sorry."

That afternoon David's class all had their heads bowed over their desks, working silently on a writing assignment, when Jesus returned after seeing Schneider. David looked up as Jesus closed the classroom door behind him. He had never seen Jesus with a smile on his face before.

David motioned him over to his desk.

"What happened?" David asked.

"He talked to me."

"That's it? He talked to you?"

Jesus just stared at David, the smile still on his face.

"Go sit down," David said. "We're not done with this yet."

Every student watched Jesus take his seat and then they all looked back at David.

"Get back to work," David said. "Please."

He sat down at his desk and then immediately stood up.

"Jesus. Everyone is writing a page describing their first memory. Start."

David walked over to the window and looked out across the red cinder track and the playing field that provided a green sanctuary amid the dirty brownstones, graffiti sprayed walls and boarded up storefronts of a Bushwick that had never recovered from the riots and burnings of the seventies. Which one of those tenements did Jesus live in?

David wished he had an adult sized, leather harness like the one his mother had used to strap him to the banister after one of David's tantrums had gone too far out of control for his mother to handle. She'd kneel down and hold him tightly while she fastened the heavy metal clasps on the leather vest that bound his chest and shoulders. No matter how hard he struggled, he couldn't escape her hold.

She'd take a leather dog leash, clamp it to the back of the vest, and then tether him to the heavy pillar at the bottom of the stair's banister. He could only move forward a few inches and he couldn't reach around to undo the clasp on the leash. Only when he had stopped his wild, thrashing movements and had calmed down enough to slide quietly down onto the floor would his mother come back and set him free.

David thought he could use one of those leashes now to fasten Jesus to the radiator so he couldn't harm the other kids.

When David had "acted out" as a child -- as they called it then -- in school, before he'd learned to control himself, his teacher would just call his mother, and she'd begrudgingly go over to the school and bring him home for the rest of the day. He knew he was the only one like that in school, but the teachers knew his parents were respectable. His father was a lawyer, after all. They could afford to cut David and his family a little slack.

What would they do with him now? What would they do with him here, today? He'd probably be sent to a foster child institution somewhere.

Maybe that's where Jesus should be, he thought. David knew that Jesus came from a home of eleven other siblings, and probably almost as many fathers, none of whom ever stayed long. Maybe a five-day suspension would be punishment enough to wake him up a little bit. Maybe he'd just see it as a reward, though. A week on the streets without a truant officer coming after him. He'd be free.

David knew the suspension might not have any effect on Jesus at all, but it was the rule. Schneider should have sent him home. It'd be an example to the other kids, too, especially the borderline rowdy ones, and it would have restored David's authority in the classroom. He felt angry, but Michelle was at work and Karen was in grad school today. There wouldn't anyone to talk to later.

David watched a train of graffiti sprayed subway cars roll across the El on the other side of the playing fields while his kids wrote quietly behind him. Through the window he could hear the deep rumble of the wheels rolling across the track couplings and he imagined he could even feel the vibrations from the heavy rail cars in the linoleum floor underneath his feet. He'd never noticed them or the subway noise before. He was always so focused on the students.

Once the train had passed, he felt the silence in the room, a presence as palpable as his own. He stood there feeling isolated from the classroom of students behind him. Funny, he thought, to feel so lonely in a room full of children. His children.

Suddenly the heavy metal door to the classroom opened with a loud whoosh that echoed down through the hallway behind it, and Schneider strode into the classroom. David heard quiet gasps from some of the children. Miranda sat straight up and her new pen fell out of her hand onto the floor.

David turned, his back to the window, but Schneider acted as if he wasn't even there.

"Well, students," Schneider said. "And what is Mr. Weintraub teaching you today?"

He walked over to Miranda's desk, picked up the paper on it and read the first line out loud. Miranda blushed.

"Not bad. But make sure he's teaching you right, now. Any of you have anything you're having a problem with this year?"

Jesus raised his hand.

"Yes, Jesus?"

"I started off in the back row, 'cause I can see the board better from back there. Somethin' about my eyes. But Mr. Weintraub makes me sit way up here now. I can't see."

Schneider turned and glared at David.

"Mr. Weintraub, let's put this student back where he can see the board, okay? Jesus, which was your seat?"

"That one back there in the corner."

"That's yours again from here on. Okay, Mr. Weintraub?"

David pushed his back against the tile windowsill behind him so he would have something solid to feel, something tangible to calm him down, a fact. His hands went flat back against the wall. He didn't say anything, but nodded.

"Good, then," Schneider said. "Now anyone else have any problem they haven't been able to figure out?"

Bobby Martinez raised his hand.

"Yes?"

"We need more writing paper, sir. Mr. Weintraub has to buy it out of his own pocket." He looked over at David as if he had done something worthy of praise.

"Tell you what. Come with me now to the office and I'll get you some. Any other questions from anyone?"

No one raised their hand.

"Okay, Bobby. Come with me. Mr. Weintraub, it's your class again."

The Vice Principal and Bobby walked out into the corridor and David stepped forward a couple feet.

"It's almost the end of the day," he said. "Just finish up your essays and I'll see you tomorrow."

The children all bowed their heads again over their papers and David walked slowly over to the board at the front of the classroom. He began erasing the notes for their essay that he had written on it earlier, and he stayed there slowly moving the eraser up and down from one side of the board to the other. When he reached one edge, he would start back the other way, rubbing the eraser slowly, thoroughly, waiting for school to end.

The final buzzer sounded and he heard everyone behind him shuffling their papers and picking up their books and getting up and moving toward the door. He didn't turn from the board.

Suddenly a book hit the board in front of him with a tremendous splat. As it fell to the floor, David realized he'd actually heard the rush of air by his left ear as it had sailed by his head. It had barely missed him.

He didn't have to turn around to know who had thrown it.

After school, David walked the block down to Kennedy Fried Chicken and had gotten himself a thirty-two ounce soda. He now stood huddled in the shadow of a doorway of one of the brownstones across from the front entrance of the school – I'm just like a local homey now, he chuckled to himself – waiting for Mrs. McCaffrey.

She came out right at four and David crossed the street and caught up with her before she reached the corner at the end of the playing field. At this time of the day, the subways rattled continuously along the El across the street.

David touched her shoulder as she waited to cross Broadway. She jumped.

"I need your advice. I need to know what to do next," he said and told her about the book Jesus had thrown at him that afternoon.

She looked back down along the sidewalk toward the school to make sure they were alone.

"You need to file a grievance. You know, through your union," she said.

"How do I do that?"

"You've got to get with your union rep, Ms. Petrocelli. You know, she's the Staff Developer too."

"The pretty one?"

"Yes, the pretty one. You've got to be careful with some of these union reps, though. They're known to do a lot of brown nosing of the school administration."

David looked at her blankly.

"You know what 'brown nosing' is, David?"

"I've heard of it."

"It's, well, it's sucking up to someone to get something out of them. Some union reps do it a lot on their way up through the ranks so they can exchange favors with school officials when they need to. I'll scratch your back if you scratch mine kind of thing, you know."

"Does Ms. Petrocelli do that?"

"Well, she's certainly got the looks for it."

When David got home to his apartment, he called his sister Karen.

"Can I come over for dinner tonight?" he asked as soon as he heard her answer the phone.

"Hi, David. Uh…"

"Are you having anything good?"

"I don't know yet. Howard's here."

That was good, David thought. Howard liked the Yankees.

"I'll be there in half an hour," he said and hung up before she could say anything else.

He had thought about just staying home by himself, but he had decided on the train home that he'd rather visit Karen. Not to tell her anything, just to be around her.

When he arrived, she gave him a hug at the door and he shook Howard's hand when he stood up from the sofa where he'd been watching the basketball game on TV. David saw the two large pizza boxes on the counter between the living area and the kitchen of Karen's studio apartment.

The three of them sat side by side on the bar stools with their slices. David was in the middle, and he and Howard swapped their enthusiasm about how the Yankees had just swept the World Series by keeping San Diego from winning even one game.

After Karen cleaned everything up, she and Howard cuddled up together on the sofa and David sat on the leather ottoman, facing them. He felt better, almost composed.

"There's a pretty woman I'm going to meet at work tomorrow," David said. "Ms. Petrocelli. She's smart, too, I think. She might be a year or two older than me."

"Oh?" Karen said.

"Yeah, it's been awhile." David knew his only girlfriend, really, had been Rosemary Feinstein for three and a half weeks when he was thirteen. "Do you suppose she's been with a lot of men already?"

"It's always hard to tell," Howard said.

Karen slapped him on the shoulder.

"Well, how many men do you suppose Michelle has been with," David asked. "She's about Ms. Petrocelli's age."

"Michelle, our sister?" Karen said. "I don't know David, what do you think?"

"A couple dozen?" David threw out.

"I think far less than a couple dozen."

"What about you then, Karen? Maybe half a dozen?" David asked.

Howard turned and looked expectantly at Karen, a big smile on his face.

"Only half a dozen? Heck, no! Shame on you, David. You should know better. I've been with hundreds. Maybe thousands."

A grin slowly appeared across David's face.

"How about you, David," Howard asked. "How many women have you been with?"

"Oh, two or three," David said.

"David," Howard said, "if it's only been two or three, you'd know which it was. Two. Or three."

"It was a while ago," David said. "You know."

"What kinds of things did you do with them?" Howard asked.

Karen shot Howard a disapproving glare and David saw her poke him in the ribs quickly with her elbow. David thought he'd better come up with a good answer.

"I ate a potato chip off a woman's breast once," he said.

"Really?" Howard said.

"It was Nancy Williams," Karen said. "She was over at my place one night, sprawled out on my sofa eating potato chips. We were just hanging out, watching a video. David had dropped by. She had spilled some chips on her chest and stomach and David bent over and grabbed the one from her breast between his teeth. She had on a wool sweater."

"It was very exciting," David said.

"I bet," Howard said.

"Howard, how do you think I should approach Ms. Petrocelli?"

"I don't know. Have you talked to her yet?"

"Not yet."

"Well, saying hello is always a good start. Hard to get rejected if you're just saying hello."

"Okay. I have to file a grievance with her, though. She's the union rep."

"File a grievance?" Howard said. "That's a great opening gambit. Nice fresh approach. Go for it."

"Stop it," Karen said.

"No, I mean it," Howard said. "Really, I do."

"Thanks." David said to Howard. "I know you do."

The next morning David put on a new blue button down shirt – the one he had been saving for Thanksgiving dinner – and made sure his Dockers were ones he had not worn before. He considered polishing his shoes, but he thought it might be better not to appear too overanxious with her. He didn't think he had any polish anyway.

But he did have his cannon.

He arrived at school early and went up to his classroom to put his briefcase down and have his Pepsi before he went up to Mrs. Petrocelli's office to start the grievance procedure.

He opened the heavy door of his classroom and walked over to his desk. A business envelope with his name typed on it had been placed on the flat surface of the desk right in front of his chair. He sat down and opened it up. It was from the Vice Principal.

"I have met with many parents from your class this month. Some students have alleged that you are physical with them. As you know, physical contact is not allowed in

New York City Public schools. That is tantamount to alleged corporal punishment charges, and during my subsequent investigation, I found that a pattern for that exists with you.

Attached please find the written policy regarding Corporal Punishment, which was distributed at our October Staff Conference. Our guidance counselors also discussed this at other meetings and they have spoken about the procedures you need to adhere to for avoiding any kind of physical contact which you might initiate.

- Charles L. Schneider, Vice Principal, PS 232"

CHAPTER 3

David didn't make it to Ms. Petrocelli's office that morning.

Instead, he sat at his desk, going over the letter from Schneider and wondering what child could possibly have complained about him. More importantly, what parent? Or parents?   Whatever the specific charge was, it was false. He'd never used any force on a student, never slapped one, never touched them any way he wasn't supposed to. He'd never touched them at all, period.

Should he make a complaint about a false accusation as part of this grievance, or would he have to do a separate grievance just for this? Maybe there was some other procedure he should use to attack Schneider for this fraudulent accusation. Something with more bite to it than a grievance.

Ms. Petrocelli would know.

After his class had ended and he'd answered Miranda's questions about the next day's writing assignment, he packed his briefcase and made his way downstairs to Ms. Petrocelli's office, just two doors down from Schneider's. He paused for a second in front of her dark wood door, but then pushed it open and walked into the little office. Ms. Petrocelli looked up from behind her desk, startled, and then stood, more to defend her space than to greet David. He was surprised how tall she seemed, close up.

"Ms. Petrocelli. David Weintraub. I need to file a grievance. Maybe two. Against the Vice Principal, Mr. Schneider."

"Why don't you have a seat, Mr. Weintraub."

She gestured to a wooden chair at the side of her desk. Her hair was full and dark and cascaded down to her shoulders and her charcoal grey sweater.

"You can call me David," he said and bumped into the back of the chair as he tried to go around it. She looked even prettier close up, as well, David realized.

"What's the nature of your grievance, Mr. Weintraub?"

David rattled off, almost verbatim, the pertinent section of the discipline code regarding endangering other students or teachers and then he described his two attempts to get Jesus either reprimanded or suspended for throwing books and erasers in class, all to no avail.

"Schneider even came into my class afterwards and moved Jesus' seat to the one he asked the Vice Principal for. I'd moved him out of it weeks before so I could keep a better eye on him. Schneider's a weasel. He's trying to undermine my authority in the classroom."

"We're going to have to leave 'weasel' out of this, Mr. Weintraub. The grievance procedure is a formal one and there's a certain protocol we'll have to use to file it."

Ms. Petrocelli reached into the bottom drawer on her right and pulled out a manila folder full of forms.

"You can call me David."

She ignored the invitation.

"Now, here's the form you're going to need to fill out. You write up what happened, state why it's an offense to the school code, and then suggest what you think is a just resolution to your grievance. Make two copies, keep the original, give me the other two and I forward one to the Superintendent at the District Office. He's got to respond to me as your union rep. If he reverses the offense, I let you know and it's over. If he doesn't, you have the right to send it up to a Board of Education rep. If they don't recognize your grievance as valid, an actual hearing is called and the matter is discussed between you, Mr. Schneider and a union ombudsman. Sometimes that's me."

She pulled the top form out of the folder and handed it to David.

"How long does this take?" David asked.

"It's hard to say."

"But what do I do in the meantime?"

"That's up to you, Mr. Weintraub."

"There's another matter, as well," David said.

Ms. Petrocelli waited for David to tell her, but he had stopped speaking and fiddled with the mimeographed form she'd handed him.

"What's that, Mr. Weintraub?"

"Schneider's accused me of inappropriate physical contact with one of my students. Maybe with more than one. Either way, it's false." His voice rose into anger as he talked.

He took the envelope he'd found on his desk out of his briefcase, slid the paper out of it and handed it to Ms. Petrocelli.

She unfolded it and read it slowly. David stared at her as she read through it a second time. Although her lipstick had worn off sometime during the day, her lips still looked quite red to David.

"This could be a serious charge, David." She started to reach a hand towards David, but then pulled it back and clasped both her hands together on her desk in front of her. "Who are these parents?"

"I have no idea. I don't even know if they exist. I told you Schneider's a weasel."

"If you're going to accuse Mr. Schneider of making a false accusation against you, that's also going to be a serious charge. Are you sure that's what you want to do? There might be another way to handle it."

"What other way? He's falsely accused me. That's not right. He's got no proof."

"He's got those parents," Ms. Petrocelli said.

"But they're lying."

"Even if they are, how can you prove that? All I'm saying is that you need to be very careful what you might get yourself into here. It could be a no win situation."

David slumped down in his chair and slid his hands deep into his Dockers pockets. He rotated the tin cannon between his right thumb and index finger as he weighed what Ms. Petrocelli had just told him, as if he were calculating the odds after being hit by the Texas Hold'em dealer with a seven and two eights on the flop when he only had a queen and a six in the hole.

"This isn't right, Ms. Petrocelli," he said after a few seconds. "I've got no choice. You just need to tell me what's the best way to go about it. What form do I need to fill out? Have you got a Bureaucratic Weasel Complaint form?"

He smiled what he thought was a particularly debonair smile at Ms. Petrocelli. She had begun to smile, too, but quickly became serious again.

"Mr. Weintraub, my suggestion would be to file the first grievance now and get it resolved before you file the second regarding the false accusation. If you're lucky, the Superintendent will respond to the first quickly and that can be over and done with before you begin the second. I think you need to keep these situations separate."

David was silent for a minute, his hands still buried in his pants pockets.

"Alright," he said, finally. "I'll bring you the first grievance, typed up, before school tomorrow morning."

"I promise I'll get the Superintendent's copy to him tomorrow. Then we'll just keep our fingers crossed." Ms. Petrocelli leaned back in her chair to signal their meeting was done.

"If you can give me your telephone number," David said, "I'd like to call you up sometime." He smiled at her again.

"Well, Mr. Weintraub, that's very sweet of you, but I think we'd better just keep the two of us as union rep and union member at the moment."

She stood and put out her hand for him to shake.

He stood slowly, trying to conceal the hurt, and the surprise, on his face, and then shook her hand.

"I'll see you first thing in the morning then," he said to her.

"That will be fine. At some point, too, we should get together and work out the career development steps you'll need to take this year. I'm the school Staff Developer."

"Cool!"

As David backed out of the door of Ms. Petrocelli's office and into the hallway, he heard a sharp "Watch it!" just before he felt the body of the person he had backed into.

He turned. Ut-oh. Dr. Harrison, the principal.

The first time David had seen her, when she had made her brief welcoming remarks to the staff in the little theater at the beginning of the school year, he had thought for a second she was the woman who had sat next to him at the job fair. Maybe not quite as large, but same dress, same hair, same attitude.

"Mr. Weintraub," she said to him as he faced her in the hallway, "Usually we walk facing forward around here so we can see where we're going."

"Excuse me, Dr. Harrison. I was just saying good-bye to Ms. Petrocelli."

"And you'd rather look at her than me, I suppose."

David was surprised to hear that, but he was already preparing to defend himself from backing into the principal.

"No, Mrs. Harrison. I've been going backwards my whole life, actually. I was a breach baby. Even tried to be born backwards," David said and laughed. It was true. He had been a breach baby, blue faced and screaming, and he'd always wondered how the oxygen he'd lost in those first minutes of his life might have affected him.

Harrison was brushing off her bosom with a fluttering hand, as if a little swarm of insects had landed on her.

Mrs. McCaffrey had told David in one of their private chats that Harrison had once told some students' parents that "those white teachers" just came in from the suburbs and didn't really work that hard, didn't really care for their kids, but she did. "I'm one of you," she would tell them.

David wondered if she had been outside Ms. Petrocelli's door, listening in, as David had talked about the Vice Principal, but he decided that couldn't have been the case. He was just being paranoid.

He hoped.

"Getting some after hours staff enhancement with Lisa today, are we?" Mrs. Harrison asked him.

"We talked about setting up a training plan for me, yes," David said.
"Have you had any in-class observations yet, Mr. Weintraub?"
"Not yet, no."

David had read in the introductory teaching packet he'd been given when he was hired that he was entitled to watch other teachers give sample lessons in his classroom and that his own lessons would be observed at some point as well. Mrs. Pavlak, the reading consultant, had given a few short math and reading lessons in his class earlier that fall, but no one had observed him teaching yet.

He was proud of what he'd already been able to accomplish with his students by himself. After a rough first few weeks of alternating between praising them and verbally disciplining them, he'd been able to establish a pretty orderly classroom – except for Jesus – and while probably only one or two of his students were college bound, they were learning what he taught. Their quiz scores showed it.

Figuring out what his students needed was kind of like figuring out a Pac-Man game, David thought. When he was seven, he had gone through every Pac Man sequence for every level and memorized how to beat the game anytime, anywhere. Only once, on a family vacation at St. Maartens, did he find a Pac-Man that he couldn't be beat. "This one must be a black market machine," he told his father.

Jesus was kind of like a black market machine, David thought. All his other students worked well under his teaching. They'd even come to like him. Except for Jesus.

"I'll have a class observation set up for you then," Harrison said. "Mr. Schneider will be in touch with you."

"Great."

"Now, you better get out of here PDQ or that union rep you just saw is going to write you up for working more hours than your contract allows."

Dr. Harrison smiled as she walked away, but David did not feel he'd just been befriended. He stood and watched her as she took a few steps down the hallway and turned into Mr. Schneider's office.

Tuesday of the following week David was sitting in the teacher's lunch room, just about to bite into the turkey club sandwich he'd gotten from the local bodega, when Miranda Gonzalez looked in through the open lunch room door, smiled and waved a note back and forth at David. He got up and took it from her. Ms. Petrocelli wanted to see him after his last class that afternoon.

"Come in, David, and close the door behind you, please," Ms. Petrocelli said after David had stuck his head around the frame of her open door. She stayed in her seat, but pointed at the empty chair next to her desk.

"Do we have news?" David asked her as he walked over to his chair.

"We do. And it's good." She handed him a typed letter from the district superintendent's office. It acknowledged that Schneider should have taken more action, and quickly, after Jesus' first throwing incident and David was thanked for bringing the infraction to the district office's attention.

"What does this mean will happen?" he asked.

"Usually a letter noting your grievance and the superintendent's response to it is placed in the offending teacher's personnel file, in this case, Mr. Schneider's."

"Is that all?"

"That's all. But it means we can file your other grievance now about the false accusation."

She reached into her bottom drawer, pulled out the manila folder and handed David a mimeographed form.

"Does this mean they're scared of me?" David asked.

"You mean, because they resolved this so quickly? Could be. By the way, I heard about Mr. Nutthauser," she said as she slid the form across the desk to David.

"Yeah, he only lasted about fifteen minutes before my kids ate him up. He came in to do his math coordination teaching and he was so boring and so condescending that they just started carrying on with each other and ignoring him until he finally walked out. It was pretty funny, really."

"Unless you were Mr. Nutthauser," Ms. Petrocelli said and laughed.

"Right." David looked over at her as he measured his next words. "I heard your first name is Lisa. How about if I call you by your first name?"

"I think I could live with that, David."

"I'll see you first thing in the morning then. With this." David took the form off the desk and rolled it tightly into his hand as he stood. He knew there was something else he should probably say before he left, but nothing came to his mind.

Just before he pulled her door shut, he wiggled all the fingers of his left hand at her to say good-bye.

Mr. Schneider opened the door to David's classroom and called David over.

"I'll be doing your in class observation next Wednesday, right after lunch, fifth period." He glanced around the classroom. "You really need to bring that bulletin board up to date, David. It looks the same as the last time I was in here. See you Wednesday."

David spent the entire weekend preparing his lesson on the influence of the Mayan civilization and had asked Mrs. Pavlak to be present during

Schneider's observation. He knew he should have an unbiased party present as a witness, if possible, in case he needed to refute any of Schneider's points in the report the vice principal would write up after his observation. Mrs. Pavlak would do.

By Sunday night David had pored over every book he could get from his local library on the Mayans, had reviewed every school recommendation on this type of reading lesson and had practiced his delivery of the individual components of his lesson in the bathroom mirror over and over again.

Still, he wasn't satisfied. His lesson had to be perfect.

After school on Monday he got with Mrs. Pavlak and went over his lesson plan. She liked it, but made suggestions to make it conform more to what she knew the school's written expectations were.

David called in sick Tuesday morning so he could continue preparing for Wednesday's class.

Wednesday morning, after the first bell rang, David prepared his class for what to expect in the fifth period and asked for their best cooperation. Miranda and Bobby Martinez assured him they'd be model students, bright and interested, and when David asked Jesus if he could please refrain from throwing anything during that hour, he nodded his head silently in assent.

After lunch Mr. Schneider arrived and sat down at David's desk while Mrs. Pavlak, who had arrived several minutes earlier, stood at the back of the classroom. In her early fifties, she was so tiny her body looked frail next to the huge bulletin board, but her emphatic nod of approval to David when Schneider walked in showed her true strength.

David launched immediately and enthusiastically into his presentation.

An hour later, he was sure he had nailed it.

He hadn't had to hesitate in his presentation on any of the information about the Mayans or the other cultures they affected or at the switches from film to written to live aspects of his lesson. Two or three times, while a film snip was playing or the students were writing, he managed to catch Mrs. Pavlak's eye at the back of the room and each time she nodded her head up and down and smiled. He was doing well.

After the lesson ended, Mr. Schneider stood up and addressed the students, who immediately had gone silent when he rose from David's desk.

"Mrs. Pavlak will take over the class for the next period while I speak to Mr. Weintraub. He'll be back to wrap up the last class of the day. Come with me, Mr. Weintraub."

David followed him downstairs to his office and then winked at Mrs. McCaffrey and stuck his right thumb in the air quickly as they passed by her desk into Mr. Schneider's inner office.

"Have a seat, David," Schneider said. He shuffled through the notes he'd taken during

class on the yellow legal pad he always carried around with him and then set the pad down

on the desk in front of him for reference.

David sat on one of two heavy wooden chairs facing his desk.

"So, the object of your lesson today was to teach how to draw conclusions by using examples of how the Mayans contributed to the culture of other civilizations. Yes?"

"Yeah! Awesome wasn't it?"

"David, that's going to be more my role to decide, I'd say, than yours. I'm going to go over with you now my responses to your class and then I'll write up those observations and have them placed in your file. Understood?"

"Yes. Easily," David said. He'd been trying to stare directly at Schneider since he had first sat down in front of him, but Schneider seldom returned his gaze directly.

"As for the development of your lesson, I observed you going over the day's new vocabulary, having the students use the words learned in sentences and then handing out the worksheets with more information about the Mayans and their culture. You then showed a video and afterward asked students individually about how Mayans contributed to other civilizations. Answers included parades, festivals, astronomy and charts for the solar system. You also went over how the planting sequence Mayans used, compared to the Hopis and the Russian farmers, before you handed out a final sheet that reinforced all you'd presented. Does that about cover it?"

"Well, I also…" David began.

"I know there were other aspects to the lesson, David. I'm just trying to be sure you agree with the general comments I'll be making about your lesson. It's only a brief overview that I'm required to make in my report."

"In that case, so far, so good."

"Now, as far as your classroom management goes, there's a couple points I should mention. First, you shouldn't be allowing students to use the bathroom during the reading block. Second…"

"Wait," David interrupted. "Mr. Schneider. No student was excused to go to the bathroom last hour."

"I know, but I've seen you do that before. I have the dates here somewhere." He reached for the yellow pad to his left and started ruffling through pages. "I can't seem to find them, right off the bat. I'll get them before I write the actual report, which, by the way, you will get a copy of. Okay. Second point, a print rich environment did not exist in your classroom today. Most of your charts were store bought. Computer generated titles would be more appropriate and uniform."

"I had to buy some of those charts myself. The school doesn't provide them. Without them, the kids would have nothing."

"Third point, your room is set up in rows, as requested."

Schneider looked up and finally returned David's gaze.

"My chairs and desks are going to be making out better in your report than I am, it sounds like," David said.

"David, are you just trying to be amusing here?"

"I am amusing, sir."

Schneider looked back down at the notes he'd taken during his observation.

"These will be my recommendations, then. First, you should just focus on one media at a time. For instance, you should stop the video and refer to the map and then restart the video."

"Hey, I agree. Good point, Vice Principal."

"Second, your vocabulary chart should have been in the center of the board and then it should have been moved after it was used."

"So, it didn't fare as well as the chairs and the desks, eh?" David smiled, but he continued to stare directly at Schneider.

"This meeting we're in, the meeting itself, to go over my observation is not part of my report – yet – but if it were, I might be including insubordination in it."

"Understood. Sir."

"Finally, your lesson should have focused on one skill, drawing conclusions, but you attempted to bring in other points of deduction and induction, so your lesson did not fulfill that requirement."

"I'd been over deduction and induction with them last week as part of a math lesson, so I was just following up and reinforcing that earlier lesson," David said.

"Be that as it may, I am going to ask Mrs. Pavlak to work with you to correct the shortcomings I observed today and to prepare you for your next observation. Meanwhile, I'm going to report that the lesson I observed was unsatisfactory."

Schneider sat back in his chair and now looked directly at David.

"You've got to be kidding!" David was almost yelling and his face had gone red as he stood. "Unsatisfactory?"

He brought himself to his full height in front of Schneider's desk. He had clenched his fists and Schneider noticed David's hands were trembling ever so slightly.

"David, I do know that you've recently become acquainted with your union's grievance procedure. You have recourse to that again if you find something disagreeable in my report. You do know that, don't you?"

"I do know that. Are we done here?"

"We're done."

David walked out the door of Schneider's inner office and past Mrs. McCaffrey without saying a word to her.

The next morning David had to escort his students down to Ms. Fontagne's classroom for their weekly music lesson. It was his last period before lunch on a half school day because the afternoon was designated a Professional Enhancement Day for the teachers of P.S. 232.

"Bobby, you can be the line leader today, okay?" David said as he gathered his students together at the door of his classroom. Bobby scooted over to the doorway and motioned for the other students to form up behind him.

David didn't like the prospect of any interaction with Ms. Fontagne, however brief it might be. The second week of school Mr. Schneider had asked David to roll a piano into the classroom she was using that day and he did, but when Fontagne arrived she discovered the piano, which she didn't want in her classroom, found out who had moved it and stormed into David's classroom and demanded, in front of his students, that he get "that useless piano out of my classroom."

David had refused and she stormed back out of his classroom, threatening to expose to anyone and everyone she could find, including the Vice Principal, his refusal to cooperate. David never heard any more about it, but he'd remained gun shy of Ms. Fontagne ever since.

April Fontagne, he mused as his class lined up behind Bobby at the door. Sounded more like a cabaret singer than the hootenanny folk singer she was reputed to have been. She was in her fifties now and wore her hair in a tight, Afro-like cut even though it had turned largely grey. David had once noticed on the pale skin above her shirt collar the colorful head of a peacock she had tattooed on the back of her neck. Below her collar it must have covered all of her back with its plumage.

As far as he was concerned, though, there was very little "peace, love and groovy" to her personality, he thought to himself, as he opened the classroom door and motioned for Bobby to lead the children down the hallway to the stairs. David followed along at the end of the line of chit-chatting students.

Bobby led the little parade fifth graders down the stairs and onto the hallway of the floor below where Fontagne's music room was. He knew enough to march up to the door of her room and keep the line behind him against the tiled wall of the hallway. Then he peeked in the doorway to let Ms. Fontagne know they'd arrived.

The line stretched out behind him along the wall and wrapped back into the stairwell with the last four students. David was with them, but he peeked down the hallway for a second to make sure everyone was next to the wall and not scattered around in the hallway.

He saw Mr. Schneider come out of the room across the hallway from the music room with Mrs. Morgan, point to David's students and lean over to say something in her ear. Just then Ms. Fontagne came out into the hallway and told Bobby to lead everyone back into her music room. She looked across at Mr. Schneider, who nodded at her before he went back into Mrs. Morgan's room. Mrs. Morgan glanced down the hallway again, saw David watching her, and then followed Schneider into her classroom.

David knew there was something unusual about what he had just seen, but he couldn't figure out the significance of it as he walked back up to his classroom after he was assured his students had been moving satisfactorily into Ms. Fontagne's music room.

In his room he packed up his paperwork for that day from his desk and stuck it in his briefcase and then walked down to the local bodega for a turkey grinder with sautéed peppers, a bag of Doritos and a large cherry cola. They mixed the cola there themselves and whoever prepared it for the seltzer hose had an extremely heavy hand with the syrup. It was the sweetest, strongest David had ever had. He loved it.

The first of the teacher enhancement meetings had been scheduled for after lunch that day and was going to be conducted by Principal Harrison in the theater. David walked down the left aisle along with the other teachers and sat right in the first row, center, just below the microphone stand set up at the center of the stage. He sipped his cola and listened to the general hubbub behind him as the teachers waited for the principal's arrival.

Fifteen minutes later Dr. Harrison walked out on the stage. Mr. Schneider and Mrs. Pavlak followed her and stood by the curtain at the left of the stage as Harrison walked over to the microphone stand, picked it up and moved it far over to the right side of the stage and walked back to the center to speak.

"This is not going to be pleasant," she started off.

David was surprised how she could make her voice carry across the room even though she was not speaking that loudly. Maybe it was just the anger in it, he thought.

"The results from the school-wide practice reading tests that were given last month have come in. Your scores are atrocious. They actually make me sick to my stomach. As a whole, the school has the lowest scoring in our district and is just barely above the bottom of all New York schools. You've got a lot of work to do and I expect you to start in on it tomorrow. I won't have this kind of bottom of the barrel scores on our next reading tests, scheduled for next March. I don't know what you've been doing during your reading lessons, but it sure hasn't been teaching reading."

45

David knew that half the people in the room did not even teach reading. They were specialists in math or science or art or, like Ms. Fontagne, music. Why was Harrison berating everybody there?

"There was only one grade level in the school that did well," she continued. "The fifth grade. That's because the fifth grade has some good teachers in it. Well, maybe except for one or two anyway. Well, actually, except for just one."

David thought she had looked right down at him for a second, but he wasn't sure. He kept looking straight ahead as she continued on because he felt sure that if he looked around behind him, he'd find every face in the room staring at him. He knew his head was already higher than anyone else's in the front row, but he refused to scrunch himself down into his seat and disappear.

After Harrison had finished speaking and had walked off the stage with Mr. Schneider and Mrs. Pavlak in tow, David stood and began shuffling out along with the rest of the teachers and staff.

As he reached the end of the first row and turned to move up the aisle, shoulder to shoulder with everyone else, he felt a hand grab his elbow from the second row as they passed it. It was Mrs. McCaffrey.

"Here," she said. "I printed this out for you." She pushed a folded piece of paper at him and then turned and made her way back down the row to join the line of teachers making their way up the other aisle of the theater auditorium.

Back in his classroom David sat down at his desk and opened the paper. It listed the reading test scores for each grade and class in the school. As a group, the fifth grade classes were the only ones in the school that had scored in the acceptable range, but their overall score had been brought up into an acceptable range by one class where every single student was reading at a fifth grade level. Mrs. McCaffrey had underlined in red that teacher's name.

"Weintraub."

As soon as David got back to his apartment that night, he called his sister Karen.

"How about I pick up a pizza and come over and we'll play Scrabble all night?"

"Can't, David. Got a big marketing test tomorrow."

"Okay. How about I pick up a pizza and come over and help you study for your big marketing test tomorrow?"

"Normally, I'd say yes, but I've still got to read the last three chapters my textbook before I even begin studying. It's going to be an all nighter."

"Wish I could help."

"I know you do. Thanks."

"Have you talked to dad recently?" David asked.

"Couple weeks ago," Karen said.

"How is he?"

"Fine. Why?"

"Everything the same?"

"Far as I know. Why, David?"

"I haven't talked to him for a while, but I need some legal advice."

"Give it a shot. He still doesn't bite."

"I'm going to. Good luck on your marketing test."

David hung up the phone and immediately dialed his father.

"Hello?"

"Hi, dad. How are you?"

"Well, long time no hear," his father said.

"Ditto."

"Are you still down there saving all those underprivileged youth in the inner city?"

"Teaching in Bushwick, yeah. Dad, I've got a legal question for you."

"Shoot."

"If I'm an employee of the city, am I still allowed to sue them? You know, sue the Board of Education?"

"So you're going to reform the whole school system while you're down there, too? Hold their feet to the fire, eh?"

"Something like that, dad. Can I sue them?"

"Not really my area of expertise, David. You're serious about this, right?"

"Quite."

"Okay, let me do a little research, call a couple people and I'll let you know what you can and can't do. How fast do you need to know?"

"Probably pretty soon. Next week or so?"

"Let me see what I can find out. Meanwhile, sounds like you better keep your eyes open down there."

"They're wide open, dad. Thanks."

Before he left his apartment for school the next morning, David made sure he had his Monopoly token in his pocket. He still didn't like the cannon or what it stood for. He'd much rather use the top hat, like a magician performing card tricks in front of a mesmerized audience, but he knew, other than his class, that wasn't going to happen at P.S. 232.

A soon as classes had broken for lunch, he went downstairs to the Vice Principal's office. Schneider's desk had one of the three telephones in the school which teachers were allowed to use to make outside calls during the day.

"Thank you, Mrs. McCaffrey," David said to Schneider's secretary as soon as he walked into the office, "for printing out the reading test results for me Friday."

"It's always nice to know the truth, David, isn't it?" she said.

"Regardless if it's good or bad, eh?"

"I guess so." She seemed unsure what David had meant, but went on, "I see your boy Jesus has gotten himself into more trouble now."

"He wasn't in class this morning. What happened?" David asked.

"He was crazy enough to steal and destroy the principal's beeper last week, but dumb enough to get caught doing it."

"Who caught him?"

"Mr. Schneider. Stomping it to shreds in the stairwell. He gave Jesus a five day suspension."

"He did?"

"Well, it was the principal's beeper, after all." She paused to be sure David had grasped her sarcasm. She thought he had. "Of course, she was the one who left it on a table in the lunch room Friday in the first place. Schneider meets with Jesus' mother later on this afternoon."

"What for?"

"To make her pay for it, I imagine."

"Good luck on that. Do you mind if I use Schneider's phone to make a call? Is this a good time?"

"Go ahead, David. Schneider's up at the district office with Harrison."

David walked into Schneider's inner office and sat down at his desk. He picked up the receiver from the black rotary phone, dialed Karen's number and then pressed his thumb down on the button where the receiver sat before Karen's number started ringing.

"Hi," he said. "I'm calling about tonight. Should I bring pizza?"

He went on talking between the silences he inserted while he rummaged around the paperwork on Schneider's desk. Underneath a pile of papers and manila folders on the side of the desk, he found Schneider's yellow legal pad. He slipped it out from underneath and started scanning through it, page by page.

There were reminders of meetings, notes on classroom observations, budget calculations for classroom supplies and textbooks, but on almost every page David found one handwritten entry after another that started off with "Weintraub:" and then contained an hour, a date, and a description of an event or a conversation.

Yep, so much for the top hat, David decided. It's cannon time.

CHAPTER 4

"Good news, David."

Ms. Petrocelli pointed to the hard wooden chair next to her desk and David rushed over to it from the office doorway.

"Tell me," David said, out of breath.

"The district Deputy Superintendent reviewed your grievance and threw out the corporal punishment charge. That will be removed from your file. In fact, the district office called Mr. Schneider down there so they could 'go over' the situation with him."

"We've got Schneider on the run, haven't we? You know, Lisa, I've started carrying around a yellow legal pad, just like he does, and every time I see something he does that looks suspicious, I write it down on the pad. Of course, I make sure he sees me doing it. It drives him crazy! He's no longer giving me disgusted looks every time he passes me in the hallway."

"Schneider did, however, write yet another letter for your file. He said that you had apparently used poor judgment when you handled one of the situations with Jesus and he suggests you use more restraint in these confrontational moments. He doesn't exactly recommend it, per se, but he does note that you could be instructed on acceptable techniques by teachers from the teacher center, your own colleagues or even veterans such as himself. That note will go in your file."

"What situation with Jesus? How could I use poor judgment if there was no situation? It's like he's accusing me of something in general without accusing me of something specific. Are these guys all in cahoots or what?"

"Perhaps he's just trying to save face," Ms. Petrocelli said.

"His face is hardly worth saving."

"The deputy's letter rejecting Schneider's corporal punishment allegation will go into Schneider's own file too, though, you know."

"Will anybody even notice it among the reams of paper probably already in there about him?"

"Well, if he tries anything else with you, let me know, David. I'd like to keep him in check from harassing any other of our teachers. I probably shouldn't say this, but you know he has a history of falsely accusing teachers...for whatever reason."

"I think we know the reason, don't we, Lisa? He's one of those guys who tries to destroy others just to keep the spotlight off himself. He knows he's worthless."

"I do know that type, David."

"And, while I think of it, I've been meaning to ask you this again -- I'm not that type, Lisa -- are you ready to give me your phone number? You don't even have to write it down. I memorize numbers instantly. Even ten digit ones. Here, try me."

"David, there's something I should tell you again, more specifically, if you've forgotten."

"What's that?"

"It's not appropriate for you to ask me for my number at work. Against the rules, you know. Sexual harassment stuff."

David hesitated for just a second.

"Oh. Of course. I knew that. Just testing you out. No offense. If you're going to be my union rep, I want to make sure you know all the rules here."

"Thanks," Ms. Petrocelli said. "Look, David. I do want to help you out. As your union rep. I think you're being taken advantage of here, but I'm going to keep my phone number to myself. Okay?"

"Well, I'm glad we've gotten that straightened out, Lisa. You know, I wrote a poem when I was very little – I should show it to you some day – called 'Friends of Mine' and I listed all my friends, Jews, Hindus, Catholics, blacks, whites, Hispanics. Now, I'd add you. 'Cause you're a friend of mine too."

"That's sweet, David. Thank you."

David got up to leave and paused at the door to give Ms. Petrocelli his little finger wave on his way out. He wasn't sure, but she almost looked like she was sad. It's probably not easy being a union rep, he thought. Must be really hard for her to get a date.

The first Friday after the Christmas break David was sitting in the faculty lunch room. Mr. Tuttle, one of the other fifth grade teachers, had been asking David his picks for the Super Bowl, and David was finishing up an extended recitation of Elway's passing statistics and Davis' rushing numbers and arguing that the Broncos should win easily, despite having a thirty-eight year old quarterback.

Tuttle nodded thoughtfully and David started to reel off more statistics from the Bronco's previous Super Bowl win the year before when Mrs. Pavlak appeared, sparrow-like, at the lunch room door.

"David, can I speak with you a moment?" she said.

David shoved the last large bite of his hoagie into his mouth, took a slug of Pepsi and got up to go to the door.

Mrs. Pavlak was so short, he realized, walking toward her, he could probably prop his elbow on her head and still rest his chin in his hand. He thought about doing that for a second – the teachers in the lunch room would probably crack up, especially if he made one of his funny faces at them while he did it – but then he noticed Mrs. Pavlak looked terribly serious.

"What's up?" he asked her as she beckoned him out into the hallway and moved to close the lunch room door behind him.

"David, I'm going to ask you to control yourself and not get upset, even though what I'm about to tell you could be very upsetting."

She put her open hand against his elbow and waited for him to speak.

"I'll be fine. What could be so upsetting?" he asked, smiling, but he knew it would have to do with some new tactic Schneider was taking up against him.

"Promise?"

"Okay. I promise, Mrs. Pavlak."

She was still serious, he realized, and he braced himself for whatever news he was about to receive. He felt his fists trembling.

"Allegations of a sexual nature have been made against you, David," she said, quietly enough that she knew there would be no echo in the cold hallway. Several eighth grade students by the stairwell had stopped their talking to look over at Mrs. Pavlak and David.

"You know they're a lie, don't you?" David asked, his face suddenly a dark red.

"I know they may be, David, but you've got to get ready to leave the school building by three o'clock. You may be arrested. They've got somebody else to take over your class. I don't know who."

"Arrested? Are you kidding me? By whom? Without any evidence? Just some trumped up hearsay so they can fire me and get me out of their hair for good?"

"I only know there are two policemen here to talk to you. Up in the principals' office, with Harrison and Schneider. They asked me to escort you up there."

"You, Mrs. Pavlak, escort me?" Looking down at her, he started laughing. "So you can wrestle me, a dangerous felon, to the ground should I

51

try to make a break for it?" He was giggling, but Mrs. Pavlak could see the pain on his face.

"These people are insane!" he shouted and slammed the wall with his fist.

"David, you promised you'd remain calm."

She watched his eyes flicking back and forth and she could see his arms twitching, too, as he made the effort to hold himself still.

"Alright, alright. Just give me second. Please, Mrs. Pavlak."

"Okay. Let's just start walking slowly."

She'd seen the group of eighth graders start to move down the hall toward them, curious after hearing David's booming voice and seeing him pound the wall. She put her tiny hand behind his back and guided him away from the students and down the hallway toward the stairwell at the other end. His large cordovans shuffled along the floor with scraping sounds.

It was a two minute walk downstairs to the principal's office, but the million thoughts raging through David's mind made it seem like hours. Everything outside him had gone into slow motion.

Who would have accused him of anything sexual? He couldn't figure it out. He went through every girl in his class, one by one, considering her, considering her parents, if he knew anything about them, and nothing made sense. Mrs. McCaffrey had told him three weeks earlier, as one of her warnings to him, that Schneider had tried to get Maria Gonzalez's father to bad mouth David, but Maria had a good head on her shoulders, he thought. She was well intentioned. There was no way she would ever do anything like that. So, who accused him, even if Schneider had put them up to it?

His mind went to Jesus. Jesus had been placed in another class after his suspension and David hadn't seen him since then, except in the hallways or the student lunch room. And Jesus was a male. The thought hit him, that kind of sexual assault? You gotta be kidding me. No way. There was no way that would stick. But still, Jesus was the most likely candidate to go after him, with or without Schneider's help.

"We're here," Mrs. Pavlak said. "Good luck, but I think everything's going to be alright in the end. There are people here who support you. Just don't get too agitated, please."

David opened the office door and walked into the principal's office.

"They're all in here, Mr. Weintraub," Dr. Harrison's secretary said and David walked through the door just behind her.

Harrison's office was huge. There were windows on two walls of the corner room and the mid-afternoon sunlight streamed in across the thick emerald carpeting and made David squint for a second as he stopped in the center of the room.

Harrison was sitting across the room from him at her large mahogany desk, polished and glistening in the sun, and Mr. Schneider was

52

standing by the window to her right, hands casually in his trouser pockets. In front of David were two uniformed New York City police officers, hats in their hands.

"Mr. Weintraub?" the older one to David's left asked. "I'm Sergeant Reilly." He had thick black hair on the top of his head which almost looked moist, but his sideburns and the hair on the back of his neck had turned white.

"Yes. You know this is a big mistake, don't you?" David said.

"I hope that that turns out to be the case, Mr. Weintraub, but before we begin talking, I have to read you your Miranda rights. Alright?"

David had heard the words from every TV cop show and every crime movie he had ever watched and they began to repeat themselves in his mind even before the officer started talking.

"Alright," he said.

"You have the right to remain silent. Anything you say can and will be used against you in

a court of law. You have the right to an attorney. If you cannot afford an attorney, one will be provided for you. Do you understand?"

"I understand."

A movement caught David's eye and he looked over toward the windows in the far wall and saw Schneider chuckling. He wanted to point at him to show the sergeant just what an evil weasel Schneider was, but he held back.

Reilly had been looking at David, puzzled, but then he spoke.

"You know, I think I've seen you at the bodega down the street, right next to our precinct, haven't I?" Sergeant Reilly said.

"Every day," David said.

"Great turkey sandwiches there, huh?"

"With sautéed peppers, my favorite."

"Me too. Now, I'm afraid there has been an allegation of sexual misconduct by you with one of your students. That student is being brought to St. Raphael's Hospital where they'll run tests for pinch marks, fluids, bruises and so forth and, depending on what they find, we'll probably want to interview you down at the precinct."

Good, David thought. Run all the tests you want to and I'll look forward to receiving an apology first thing Monday morning.

"They won't find anything. Who's the student?" David said.

"I'm sorry, but we can't give out the name of a minor, Mr. Weintraub."

"What about the name of her parents? Or isn't it a 'her'? What's their name? They're not minors, are they?"

"We can't give out their names at this point either, I'm afraid. I'm sure this is upsetting to you, but that's the way the law works."

"I don't have any objection to the law, officer," David said. "I have nothing to hide. I've done nothing wrong." He looked down at the handcuffs suspended from Reilly's thick black belt. "Are you going to arrest me now?"

"I'd prefer not to do that," Reilly said. "We do have the option of waiting for those test results to come in before we act. Is there anything you'd like to say right now, remembering what you say could be used in a court of law, if it ever came down to that."

"I just want to tell you I'm completely innocent. I've never done anything inappropriate with any of my students. Female or male. The charge is ridiculous. Do I need to get a lawyer?"

"That would have to be your call, sir."

"By the way, officer, what have the principal and vice principal said to you while you were waiting for me?" David asked.

"They're not your accusers, Mr. Weintraub. They only brought the matter to our attention after the parent met with Mr. Schneider."

"'The' parent? Not parents?"

"I believe so, yes."

"I guess that narrows it down a bit, doesn't it?"

"Mr. Weintraub, I don't think there's any need for an arrest to be made today." He turned to his partner, who nodded. "We have an allegation, that's all, and your denial. It's one of those 'his word against mine' kind of things right now. There's no evidence, no witnesses. A lot of the time these things just turn out to be a misunderstanding."

David looked across the room at Schneider and saw he wasn't even smiling, let alone chuckling.

"There will be an investigation, of course," Reilly said, "but at the moment you're free to go, Mr. Weintraub…unless the principal wants a word with you."

I'd rather talk to you cops, David thought. In fact, I'd rather talk to the Gestapo than to Harrison.

"Thank you, Officer Reilly," David said.

"Mr. Weintraub," Harrison called out to him from her desk. "I believe it'll be best for you to leave the building now, while everyone is still in last period. Plan on coming in Monday to meet me in my office at…" She looked down at the leather bound calendar on her desk. "…let's say ten o'clock."

"I'll be here. Thank you again, officer."

David reached out to shake hands with each of the officers and then turned to leave the room, his stiff arms down against his sides, each of his hands splayed out.

"Good-bye, Mr. Weintraub," Officer Reilly said as David walked away.

David called and called his father Friday night and Saturday, but only ended up leaving a series of messages on his answering machine. David wanted his legal advice. Finally on Sunday morning he called Karen, who told him his father and stepmother were in West Palm Beach for a long weekend.

David spent the rest of the day at the Bayside Public Library researching the law.

Monday morning he went into school early to speak to Mrs. McCaffrey and to take another look at Schneider's desk, if possible.

When he walked into the vice principal's office, a young woman with red hair and pale skin greeted him from Mrs. McCaffrey's desk.

"Good morning," she said with a smile.

"Where's Mrs. McCaffrey?" David asked her, ignoring her pleasant greeting.

"Oh, Mrs. McCaffrey's retired. Her last day was just before the Christmas vacation. Can I help you?"

David had hoped Mrs. McCaffrey could help fill him in on what David was certain was Schneider's behind-the-scenes collusion with whoever the accusing parent was or maybe even with Principal Harrison. But now David's ally was gone.

"No, thanks. I'm just here to use the phone. Is Mr. Schneider's office free?"

"My name's Mindy Fletcher, by the way. You're a teacher here?"

"Yes. David Weintraub. Fifth grade." At least until last Friday, David thought.

"Oh, that's fine then. Go ahead in. Mr. Schneider's over with the principal."

David made his way into the dark inner office and sat down at Schneider's desk, dialed the phone and spoke loudly into the silent receiver.

"Karen? Good morning. Hey, I need a favor," he began, the receiver propped against his ear by his shoulder while he began shuffling through the paperwork on the desk with his free hand. He couldn't find the yellow legal pad. Schneider must have it with him.

"Okay, Karen. Thanks much," he said and made a point of banging the black receiver down noisily back onto the phone.

"Thank you, Mindy," he said on his way out of the front office "Nice meeting you."

"The same."

David walked up the stairs to the second floor and went down to his class room. He wanted to see who had been assigned to his class, but the door was shut and he wasn't about to peek in. He knew it would be too disturbing for his students to see him.

It's not a very good morning, David thought, as he went back down the stairwell to Harrison's office. What does she have in store for me now? One, two, three, four, five, six, seven.

After quickly saying "good morning," Harrison's secretary went right back to what she'd been typing and ignored David. He settled down into the worn sofa facing her to wait. Harrison's office door was closed.

He lifted his briefcase to his lap, opened it up and took out a batch of writing exercises he'd given his students Friday. Using the case as a desk, he began grading the papers and making little notes on each one. No matter what happened this morning, somehow he'd get these back to his students.

Fifteen minutes later Mr. Schneider came out of Harrison's office, his yellow pad tucked under his left arm, and walked past David without saying a word. David kept grading his papers.

Five minutes later Harrison appeared in her doorway.

"Mr. Weintraub, I'll see you now," she said.

David set his briefcase on the sofa with all the papers still on top and followed Harrison back into her large office. She went around and sat down at her desk, but when David went to sit in one of the armchairs facing her, she motioned for him to come stand right at the front of her desk, like a naughty child.

"I'm told you've been having a hard time with your class, David, and so I'm going to offer you a position supervising a small group of children in the class for kids with attendance problems," she said.

"A hard time with my class?" David asked. He quickly unclasped his hands from in front of him and put them on the edge of her desk, supporting himself with his long arms. "You just got the results of the fifth grade reading tests. Did that look like I was having a problem with my kids?"

"Calm down, Mr. Weintraub, and please take your hands off my desk. I'm just trying to find you a position we'll all be comfortable with. I can't put you back in your classroom with this police investigation going on, anyway. Surely you know that. I haven't heard back from them yet, of course."

She had taken one of the brown glass beads from the bottom loop of her necklace and was rubbing it slowly and deliberately between her thumb and forefinger as if she were about to squash it.

David straightened to his full height as he realized she...they...were trying to get rid of him. If he accepted the transfer to the bad attendance class, he might be able to finish out the year with them, but he'd be accused of giving up his class – while he still had the Unsatisfactory rating from Schneider's class observation – and that would give them grounds to let him go. With the "U" rating, he'd never be able to get a teaching job again. They'd claim he'd abandoned his class because he couldn't handle it.

"I'm not giving up my class. I'll just wait until the police finish their investigation, if I have to. They're going to clear me anyhow. You know that."

Harrison let go of the bead and the necklace fell back against her white blouse.

"I see. Now, you're one of those who comes into Bushwick every morning from out on the island, aren't you?"

"Just from Queens. Bayside."

"Wouldn't you be happier teaching out there somewhere?"

"I couldn't get a teaching job out there. My resume's great, but they say I don't interview well."

"I suppose not. Even the vice principal tells me you're a bit uppity at times, Mr. Weintraub. Do you think that's true?"

"I don't know about 'uppity.' I'm just teaching my kids to observe and think for themselves -- something Mr. Schneider may not always be capable of doing himself, from my experience with him. Of course, I teach my kids to read, write and do math as well. I like my class here, Mrs. Harrison. These kids need me. I like what I'm doing here and I'm going to keep doing it."

"Alright, Mr. Weintraub. Be that as it may, tomorrow I'm assigning you to work helping out with the school nurse's office. We'll keep you there for awhile and see how that works out until the police finish their investigation."

"Doing what? Taking temperatures? Applying Band-aids? Sticking tongue depressors down students' throats? Should I wear my scrubs tomorrow?"

"Not uppity, eh? No. More likely you'll be stocking cabinets, dusting counters, filing papers. I don't think we want you near any children until this police thing is over, do we, Mr. Weintraub?"

"Why don't you just have me rake the cinders in the athletic field track then? No kids out there this time of year."

"That will be all for the moment, Mr. Weintraub. Thank you." She pulled open the top drawer of her desk and took out an envelope. "Oh. And this is for you. From Mr. Schneider. Apparently you abandoned your class one day last December."

"What?"

"Just read his report. By the way, Ms. Petrocelli, who I understand you've come to know fairly well, is out today. Assuming you might want to see her about this." She waved the envelope in the air before handing it to David.

"I'm sure I will."

David turned and walked out of the room, down the hall, out the front door and along the street to the neighborhood bodega. It was time for a turkey hoagie, with sautéed peppers, and a thirty-two ounce Cherry Cola. Maybe two.

David arrived at school early the next morning and went up to his second floor classroom. No one was there yet. He opened his briefcase and took out the papers he'd corrected for his students and laid them out across the whole surface of the desk in neat rows and columns. That way, they'd know he'd been there.

He'd never seen the nurse's office, had never had to send a student down there and had never met Mrs. Jeffreys, the school nurse, but he knew she had a reputation.

He walked down to the end of the first floor hallway, past the vice principal's and principal's offices, both with their doors closed, and made his way to the final door on the right. He knocked once but opened the door immediately. The white room was tiny.

"You're Weintraub, right?" the woman in the white nurse's uniform asked him.

"I am."

"Lordy. There's barely enough room in here for me and you're twice my size. How'd you end up getting sent down here anyway? Harrison got a bug up her butt for you?"

"Something like that," David said. "What would you like me to do?"

"Stay out of my way. So, what'd you do to end up down here?"

"I didn't do anything, but I've been accused of inappropriate conduct with one of my students."

"Doesn't surprise me a bit. The way these girls dress nowadays, anything could happen. Well, okay, then. Now, what am I going to put you to work at?" She turned towards the back counter and swung open the two cupboard doors below. "You got someplace to go? You know, if I give you stuff to do. There's no room in here."

"I guess I could go to the teacher's lunch room," David said. He was beginning to like Mrs. Jeffreys.

"Good idea. You're a smart cookie, I see. Big, but smart. Here. Take these student files. Go through each one and put 'em in date order. I just throw stuff in there. They're probably all a mess."

She pulled a thick stack of folders from one of the shelves. David was staring blankly down at her.

"Yeah, I know," she said. "Kinda like being in the Army. Busy work. Now get out of here and don't come back til lunch."

She stood up and thrust the stack into David's arms.

"Yes, sergeant," David said.

"Good. You've got a sense of humor. Gotta have here or you'd go crazy."

That's the truth, David thought.

Mrs. Jeffreys held the door open for him as he made his way out into the hallway, awkwardly balancing the folders and his briefcase together in his arms.

"I'd run out for some donuts and some coffee if I were you, mid morning. Don't rush it, either, big boy," she said as she closed the door behind him.

Later that afternoon David knocked on Ms. Petrocelli's door and waited to hear her voice telling him to come in. Instead, the door opened right up.

"David! Come in," she said.

"We've got a real fight on our hands, Lisa," David said as he rushed past her and made his way to his chair.

"What happened?" she asked. "Wait. Let me lock the door first. Just in case."

She turned the deadbolt below the door knob and then went back to her desk, sat in her chair and leaned forward toward David.

"Okay. Tell me what's happened."

David told her about the events of the last two school days and told her he'd finally managed to reach his father the night before and that his father had turned him over to Charlie Silverstein, an attorney friend of his who specialized in police matters. David had called Silverstein that morning and he was going to represent David to get the inappropriate sexual conduct charge dropped. David had been over everything with him while he was at the donut shop, where he had felt it was safe to talk.

"But I need your help in doing another grievance to get this abandonment of class letter removed from my file," he said. "That's a serious charge. False, but serious."

"Of course."

"These people are trying to force me to quit, Lisa, but if I do, I'll forfeit my legal right to sue them, and I'm not going to do that."

"I can't believe they're doing this to you. You, of all people," she said and this time did reach over and pat the back of his hand.

"I know. Crazy, huh?"

"You father's a lawyer?"

"Yes."

"Are you two close?"

"Not too much. When I was growing up, he worked a lot and I'm not sure he knew quite what to do with me. Father and son stuff, you know. I was a lot smarter than he was and that could have made it tough on him."

"Tough on you too, I bet," she said.

"I think he's going to help me out now, so that's good. You know, with the legal stuff at least. I think these people are ganging up on me. You probably think I'm paranoid, don't you, Lisa."

"No. Schneider's reputation from his last school is pretty well known around here and Harrison, well, she just wants everything to look like it's okay to the district and the Board of Education downtown. She's more of a politician than a principal. I haven't been immune from their prejudice myself, even though it's becoming politically trendy now in her eyes to have a token white person on staff. Affirmative action's all upside down here in Bushwick. I've become a feather in her cap, but I can still tell what she really thinks of me by the way she looks at me. Anyway, let's talk about how to approach this new grievance of yours."

She reached into her bottom drawer and pulled out the paperwork they'd need.

"You know, Lisa, I am ready to go to war," he said and gave her one of his practiced smiles. He reached into his pocket, pulled out the tin cannon and placed it on her desk between them. "See. My good luck charm. For war."

"That's a Monopoly token, isn't it?" she said and picked it up and turned it in her fingers, admiring it. "I remember these!"

"I want you to be the top hat," David said.

"Will that mean I'm on your team?"

"It sure will. I've got one at home. I'll bring it in to you tomorrow."

"We're in this together then, David?"

"We are."

CHAPTER 5

The next morning after David had dropped off the top hat with Lisa -- who had carefully placed it in the "special" pocket of her purse -- he made his way down the hall to Schneider's office.

"Good morning, Mindy," he said as he entered. "And how are you this fine Tuesday morning?" He knew he sounded a bit like W.C. Fields, but he wasn't sure how else to make himself seem nonchalant and carefree to her, as if nothing shady was about to occur.

"Well, hello, Mr. Weintraub."

David could see she was surprised to see him and he hoped she wasn't going to become suspicious of him using the phone again. He planned on using it a lot from now on.

"I'm fine, thank you," she added. "How can I help you this morning?"

"I just need to use the phone for a second," he said and walked on into Schneider's office.

"Oh. Help yourself," Mindy said to him over her shoulder as he passed by her.

David sat down at Schneider's desk and glanced over all the paperwork. Good, his yellow pad was right there. David reached down into his briefcase and took out one of the five disposable cameras he'd bought the night before. They were party favors for birthday partings and weddings, but they were tiny and he knew they'd be perfect for him to photograph any evidence he ran across anywhere at school.

This is kind of exciting, he realized, even though he was still nervous that someone would catch him. He looked out through the office doorway and then picked up the phone. David Weintraub, private investigator, he thought, I love it.

"Good morning, Karen," he began loudly enough so Mindy in the outside office could hear him after he'd pressed down the receiver button with his thumb.

David pulled the legal pad to him and scanned the first page notes. Nothing. He flipped the page and halfway down the next yellow sheet he saw the entry "1/7 Maria Rodriguez re: parent meeting, BCW, with Mrs. Lawrence."

He photographed it.

It struck David that if Schneider had met with Mrs. Lawrence, one of the school's guidance counselors, and with the Bureau of Child Welfare in connection with Maria Rodriguez, Jesus' mother, on the seventh of January, then Schneider's claim that the first he had heard of the allegations was on the eighth was a lie. Schneider must have conspired with the mother the day before the police had arrived at school and the accusing "parent" must have been Jesus' mother. Now David had photographic proof of that.

"Bye, Karen. See you tonight," he said into the silent phone.

David slid the camera back into his briefcase and made his way out of the office with an especially friendly "Good-bye, Mindy. Thanks!" on his way out the door.

"Oh, you're welcome, Mr. Weintraub!"

He turned left and walked down to the guidance office. He could talk briefly to Mrs. Lawrence and still be down at the nurse's office on time, he thought, as he pushed open the door of the Child Welfare office and shut it quickly behind him before anyone in the hallway could see him enter.

Mrs. Lawrence was just hanging her overcoat on the tall wooden stand next to the door and she jumped a bit as the door burst open and quickly closed.

"Mr. Weintraub!"

"Mrs. Lawrence, can I ask you a question? You know there has been an accusation against me?"

"Yes, I heard," Mrs. Lawrence said as she straightened out the bunched sleeves of her heavy white sweater after taking her coat off. "It was like a bombshell to me. I couldn't believe it."

She was only in her thirties, and pretty, but David had heard she was already getting a divorce. What was it with these women, David wondered.

"Can I ask you, did you have a meeting with Maria Gonzalez last week on the seventh?"

"That was Thursday. Yes, I did."

"And who else was there?"

"Mr. Schneider and Maria's daughter."

"Not Jesus?"

"No. Why would he be there? We only went over Carmen's – Maria's daughter's – attendance. She's in risk of staying back this year. I'm trying to help her. She's not a bad girl."

"Did my name come up?"

"Your name? Why would it? No. Not once. That's why I was so shocked when I heard the police came for you Friday."

"Schneider never mentioned me?"

"No. He escorted Mrs. Rodriguez in and escorted her out after, but I don't think he said more than one word during our meeting. It was all about Carmen."

"Thank you, Mrs. Lawrence," David said and started to leave.

He realized Schneider and Jesus' mother must have done their conspiring in the hallway before or after the meeting with Lawrence, which was probably set up as a sort of camouflage for Schneider's true purpose, the accusation against him.

Mrs. Lawrence reached over tugged on the elbow of his jacket sleeve.

"What's going to happen?" she asked.

"Good question," David said and left.

As soon as he had pulled the door shut and had started walking down the hall, he heard the echo of high heels coming from the other end of the hallway as someone came up the steps from the front doors. Dr. Harrison appeared before David could slip into the nurse's office.

"Mr. Weintraub!" she yelled.

He stopped and waited for her to walk up to him, her high heels still clicking loudly. He noticed she had gotten a new hairdo over the weekend, a tight Afro cut, and it made her head seem smaller. She was still a mighty big woman, though, David thought, as she paraded up to him.

"I've got something for you," she said and she balanced her briefcase on one knee and searched through it before pulling out two envelopes. "Ms. Fontagne and Mrs. Morgan have both written up reports about the day you abandoned your class."

"Of course they have," David said.

"I'm not sure what you mean by that, Mr. Weintraub. Anyway, these are your copies," she said and thrust the two white envelopes toward him before she walked off toward her office.

He heard her door close as he stood there in the hallway, the two envelopes dangling from his hand, down against his thigh.

"She's a piece of work, ain't she?"

David turned to his right and saw Mrs. Jeffreys standing in her open doorway. She must have cracked her door open to listen to Harrison and David in the hallway.

"Yes, she is," David said and smiled at Mrs. Jeffreys' sudden presence.

"You better get your butt in here before something else -- even worse -- happens to you out there in that hallway."

On his break that morning David decided to postpone his donuts and soda and go see Lisa Petrocelli first.

"David!"

"Top Hat!" David closed the door behind him and turned the dead bolt himself. "I don't think anybody saw me."

"Have we switched to guerilla warfare now?" Lisa asked him

She stood up and came out from behind her desk and David made his way over to her. They both hesitated awkwardly for a second, face to face, seeing if either was going to initiate a hug, but instead they sat down in their chairs.

"Have I got something to show you!" David said. He reached into his briefcase and pulled out the little black camera. "Look, Lisa. A disposable camera. I'm photographing our evidence."

Lisa took it from his hand and turned it over in her hands, examining it.

"Brilliant!" she said. "We should be playing Clue, not Monopoly."

"You could be Miss Scarlett!"

"Yes! How cool would that be? And you'd be Colonel Mustard, right?"

David stretched back in his chair and rubbed his protruding tummy like a buddha.

"Nope. I'm more of a plum, I think."

"Have you taken any pictures yet?" Lisa asked.

"Yeah, and listen to this. Schneider has a note that he met with Jesus' mom the day before I was accused of sexual misconduct. So he must have gotten her to make the accusation. I'm guessing he offered her not to have to pay for the beeper Jesus destroyed, maybe even for some of the expenses from the fire he'd started in the auditorium. Maybe he even said he'd help Jesus sister from not being held back a grade. I don't know, but something. I photographed the whole page from his yellow pad in his office this morning."

"David, be careful. What if you get caught?"

David thought for a second.

"I'd be screwed." He fiddled for a second with the little black camera after Lisa put it back into his hands. "Actually, not. If the evidence I photographed was good enough, it would trump any scolding I'd get for taking the photo, no? I mean, what are they going to do, dismiss me for taking a photo?"

"They might."

"Yeah. They might." He looked down again at the camera in his hands. "You know, I don't know if I'm playing by the rules of the game, but at least I'm playing."

David slipped the camera back into his briefcase and took out the two letters from Ms. Fontagne and Mrs. Morgan confirming he'd abandoned his class. He handed them to Lisa. She read them and then immediately pulled out two more grievance forms from her bottom drawer. They began filling them out together so they could get them removed from David's personnel file, too, along with Schneider's original accusation.

When they'd finished, David said, "You're the best."

"You too."

David gathered up all the paperwork, filed it neatly in his brief case and stood to leave.

"Thank you, Lisa."

"You know," Lisa said, "I don't know if I'm playing by the rules of the game either, but at least I'm playing too. I feel good about it. It's right."

She held her hand in the air and wiggled her fingers at him, but he had already gone out the door.

As David walked quickly down the street to the donut shop, he realized he probably did need to sue these people. What they were doing to him wasn't right, it wasn't fair. He knew he'd need his father's help, though, with a lawsuit.

David bought two Boston Cremes and a large Pepsi and went and sat down at a table in the far corner of the shop, next to the pay phone. When he finished his donuts, he stood and called his father.

"Good morning, David. What's up?" his father said after answering the phone in his office.

"I need your help in suing these bastards."

"Which bastards?"

"The ones who are trying to get me to quit being a teacher. Do we sue them for harassment, retaliation, revenge, oppression, persecution, malevolence, mental cruelty, torture, barbarism, or what? And who do we sue? The individuals? The schools? The New York Board of Education? The city? I'm ready to…"

Once David started talking, his father had to call out his name several times to get him to stop.

"David, David, David. Think for a second," his father said, once his son seemed to have calmed down. "Are you sure you want to go through with this? We don't want another episode, you know, like the one you had after your mother died. Maybe it's just best to walk away from all this. There'd be no shame in that. It's too much stress."

"Episode?" David thought. Yes, he'd snapped, gone crazy for a day or two, and then sank into months of apathy after his mother had died and after he'd heard them making fun of him at the radio station. He'd had to

65

adjust to having a new stepmother, too, a change that would affect any son. Only after his older sister, Michelle, had arrived and helped him find a counselor had his life gotten better.

But this wasn't the same. Now he was just plain angry at the injustice. Rightly angry. This wasn't the same at all.

"These people are wrong," David said into the receiver. "What they're doing is wrong. If they get away with doing this to me, they can get away with doing to anyone, to any little guy."

"But a suit is going to take some time, David. To put together, to push through the courts, to try to win. It's not an automatic thing, you know. 'The wheels of justice grind slowly,' as they say. But they do grind."

"Yeah, but while they're grinding, even slowly, they may be preventing all the other little guys from being ground up by this system, ground up til they're hamburg. I'm gonna do this. It'll help others. Are you going to help me?"

"Yes, I will. I'll meet you at my office this Saturday morning, say ten. Bring everything you've got so far. And, David, start getting everything you can from them in writing. That's important."

"I know, Dad."

"By the way, Charlie Silverstein called me yesterday. He talked to Detective Sweeney again, the guy in charge of your police case, and he's pretty sure they're just going to throw the whole thing out. Sweeney told him he thought that what's his name, Schneider, is just out to get you. But they've got to go through all their investigation steps and then write everything up. It could be April before it's over. 'The wheels of justice…' you know."

"I'll see you Saturday morning."

David hung up the pay phone.

When he got back to the nurse's office at school, Mrs. Jeffreys said Dr. Harrison had come by and wanted to see him.

'Don't let that woman mess with you," Mrs. Jeffreys told him as he turned and went back out into the hallway.

"Have I shown you my good luck token?"

"Nope."

"Here. Look at this," he said and pulled the tin cannon out of his pants pocket and held it out in his open palm in front of her. "See. I'm invincible."

"Well. That's good to know."

As David made his way down the corridor, the vice principal came out of his office, saw David, stopped and made it a point to scowl at him.

David immediately set his briefcase down on the floor, fished out his yellow legal pad and held it out in front of him with his left hand as he made notes on it with his pen. Schneider watched as David underlined his entry and tapped his pen once against the page when he was done.

The vice principal turned around quickly and walked off the other way down the hallway. David was smiling. Now on to Harrison, he thought.

"Come in, Mr. Weintraub," Harrison said to him. She was standing over by the window at the far side of her room and David wasn't sure if he should walk over to her or stop at his normal place, in front of her desk.

"You can have a seat," she said and walked back over to her desk. She sat down in the large leather chair and faced him across the cluttered surface between them.

David sat down in one of the two easy chairs in front of her desk. She had on a string of turquoise beads over her white blouse today and the fingers of her right hand played with them nonchalantly as she looked at David, gauging him.

"The District Superintendent has decided you should be waiting out the results of the police investigation over at the District Office. That's the customary place for teachers to report when they're on probation or waiting for the resolution of some difficulty. You're to report there tomorrow."

"The District Office?" David asked.

"You know, Mr. Weintraub. It's just down the street, not far from here at all. You can even still order your -- what were they? -- turkey sandwiches, for lunch at that local bodega. Report to Superintendent Menendez's office at eight tomorrow morning. It's right on the first floor."

"I'll find it, but I want you to put that transfer, and the reasons for it, in writing for me. Please."

"There's no need for that, Mr. Weintraub. At least, not from me. If you feel you absolutely must have it in writing, ask for it from the District Office. And also, when you get there, you'll need to check in with a Mrs. Bradshaw. She's the union rep for the district. We've arranged for all your grievance petitions to be transferred to her. You won't need to see Ms. Petrocelli for anything else any more. I'll let her know myself that you're done with her representing you."

David sat there silently. He hadn't expected that. The district office might not be that far away, he thought, but without Top Hat, it might as well be in a different universe. He'd be alone. She was his friend.

"You can go now, Mr. Weintrub. Pack up anything you still have here in the school. You might as well take the rest of today off. I have nothing else for you to do here."

David rose, his fists tight, and with effort held himself back from saying anything else to Harrison. Wasn't it Ghandi, he remembered, whose silent resistance ultimately won out the day against British imperialism? Yes. He'd be like Ghandi. Maybe he'd throw a little Martin Luther King in as well. Those guys would be his friends now.

Without a word he turned and walked out of her office, his heavy shoes silent on her carpeted floor.

The district offices were housed in an old, three story Victorian structure from the era when schools and prisons were both made of the same red bricks and designed by the same government architects. The bricks of the first floor were sprayed with yellow and purple graffiti, up to shoulder height, some of it surprisingly artistic, some of it just angry scrawls and signatures of this or that gang. These poor kids had become like animals, David thought, marking these bricks like dogs mark their territory by lifting their legs.

He walked up the flight of chiseled granite steps and pushed open one of the two heavy wooden doors that led into the first floor. The wide hall in front of him was empty and silent. He walked down past each doorway and read the faded black ink inscriptions on the opaque glass of the doors to figure out exactly where he was supposed to go. Halfway down on his left, he read "Superintendent's Office, Ramon Menendez" and he opened the door slowly and looked in.

A thin woman in her forties, her black hair in a severe pixie cut, looked up at David from her desk, but said nothing.

"I'm David Weintraub. Dr. Harrison sent me over here."

"Right. Weintraub," the woman spoke as she picked up the phone and pushed an intercom button.

"Mr. Weintraub," David corrected her.

"Weintraub's here," she said into the receiver. "What do you want me to do with him? Okay."

The door to the rear office opened and a short, balding man, what hair he had left pomaded to the sides of his head, walked out and extended his hand for David to shake.

"We're going to take good care of you here, David," Menendez said, "while all this police business gets wrapped up."

"I don't expect it to take long," David said. "I'm innocent. By the way, I'd like to have something in writing from you about why I'm being held here and not allowed to teach…even though there's been no evidence presented against me."

"'Being held here,' David, doesn't really describe the situation. You're free to quit anytime you want to, you know."

David had started to hope that his name could be cleared more quickly over here in the district office, away from the local collusion of Schneider and Harrison against him, but now he wondered. These people couldn't be in cahoots with Harrison too, could they?

One, two, three, four, five, six, seven.

"I don't want to quit," David said. "I want to teach. Sir."

"That's good. We need good teachers…although Dr. Harrison told me you've had some problems with your class."

"Perhaps you should talk to my students, not Dr. Harrison. My fifth grade ranked highest in reading competence at our school."

"Yes, well. I'm going to assign you to work in the computer room with Vera Rubin for the moment. Mrs. Crawford," he said to his secretary, "would you explain to Mr. Weintraub how he can get to the computer room downstairs?" He turned back to David. "You'll be just fine down there."

"Sure," David said. "When can I get something in writing from you?"

"See Mrs. Crawford about that next week," Menendez said and disappeared back into his office.

Mrs. Crawford gave David directions to the computer room in the basement and he went back out into the large hallway. It was still empty, still silent.

Where is everybody hiding, David wondered. The hallway reminded him of a Transylvanian castle in a nineteen thirties Dracula flick. Maybe everyone was still lying low from all the bad press coverage the district had gotten over the last few months, he thought.

First, a young white teacher had been accused by a black parent with connections to the school board of teaching a racist book, even though the work in question had been written by a black educator and had received national awards for its treatment of a potentially touchy ethnic subject. The teacher had immediately been removed from her classroom by Menendez and sent here to the district office. She would have been kept out of the classroom until she quit or was fired if it hadn't been for the press coverage.

Because of its controversial racial aspect, the story had made the national media too and the teachers in the district had still been talking about it when David started at Bushwick the September before.

The second round of negative publicity had come just the previous month. David had read the story himself in a local New York magazine. The article had exposed the district for taking children with Hispanic surnames and placing them in bilingual classes, regardless of their ability to speak English. The unfair tracking tactic was done, it was reported, to protect the local Hispanic middle class from any other immigrants and outsiders campaigning for their own children to get a higher quality education. The article labeled it intra-racial racism, as it discriminated by surname and nationality for the local Hispanic population.

David remembered Menendez being mentioned in that article too.

Maybe I've gone from the frying pan into the fire, David thought, as he walked down the back stairwell into the dank basement of the building. Normally he didn't trust the press, but the facts here, as reported anyway, seemed indisputable.

"Mrs. Rubin?" David stuck his head into the little room and immediately felt the dry warmth of computer-heated air. A row of six new pc's sat on two long folding tables, end to end against the right wall and across from a solitary desk.

A woman bent over a young man seated at the first computer. An older gentleman sat in the last seat down by the back wall.

"Yes. That's me," Vera Rubin said as she straightened up and faced David. She had a little smile on her face as if she were pleased to announce that that's who she was.

"I'm David Weintraub. I'm supposed to report to you. The superintendent sent me down here."

"Welcome," she said and stuck out her hand. "Have a seat over by my desk. I'll be right with you. John here got sent down too. Yesterday. He's got fingerprint problems."

John and David nodded at each other and David walked over to Mrs. Rubin's desk and sat in one of the two wooden chairs facing it.

He glanced over at the man at the back of the room and was surprised at how well dressed he was in his camel hair sport coat, crisp white button down shirt and paisley tie. He had one leg crossed over the other and David could see his charcoal slacks still had a sharp crease in them, with pressed cuffs above his shiny loafers. He sat in front of the last computer reading a novel.

Vera Rubin, a squat little woman with high cheekbones and the forearms of a wrestler, came over and sat down next to David after she had finished up with John.

"Mrs. Crawford said you could be here for awhile," she said.

"I hope not," David said. "No offense to you, of course."

"Understood." She looked at David's face for a minute, assessing, before she continued. "I'm going to set you up with the computer next to Mr. Nelson so you can go through it and see what's there. You'll be helping out staff who come down here to do work or research on our computers. You know how to use a computer, don't you?"

"I'm a pro," David said and threw her one of his practiced smiles.

"Good. Because most of the people who come down here don't know squat. I've got to be upstairs for awhile this morning. Mr. Nelson can answer any questions you have. Anthony!" she called over to the man at the far end of the room. "This is David Weintraub. He's going to be getting familiar with our computer system this morning. Help him out if he has any questions, will ya?"

The man set his novel down on the table in front of his computer.

"Of course. Glad to meet you."

David was surprised at how strong his Brooklyn accent was. He sounded more like a dock worker than a teacher, David thought, especially a teacher dressed to the nines like that. Nelson stood, ready to shake David's hand.

After Vera had left and David was sitting, letting the computer in front of him warm up, Anthony turned in his chair to face David to show he was ready for conversation.

"So you're in detention here too?" he asked.

"Detention? Yeah, I guess you could call it that. I'm just waiting for my case to be cleared up so I can go back to my classroom in Bushwick. You're not in 'detention,' too, are you?"

"I most certainly am. I'm -- or was -- a math teacher in the Gifted Middle School over on Dekalb Avenue. Now I'm apparently a computer instructor."

He spoke like a teacher, like he was educated, David thought, but his gravelly voice was still right off the streets of nineteen-fifties Brooklyn.

"How'd that happen?" David asked, even though he was pretty sure he could guess the answer.

"My life had been just fine for years and years, teaching. Then we got a new vice principal. Like our principal, he had been appointed, or at least "suggested," by Menendez. Suddenly he was writing up all of my lessons as "Unsatisfactory." One winter morning I was two minutes late to class and because I had 'allegedly' left my windows open a crack overnight, I was accused of being the cause of the pipes freezing and bursting. The way they worded it, you'd think I'd been carefully plotting the sabotage. The boys upstairs here – Menendez and his henchman – agreed with my principal and vice principal, but there was no evidence I was guilty."

"That sounds like the same thing that happened to me," David said. "Everything made up. They just wanted to get me out of the classroom."

"You got it. I refused to give up my classroom, despite their pressure, so they raised the ante. The vice principal accused me of teaching prostitution in my class. Can you believe it? My name and my picture were suddenly in all the New York papers. Now they had their reason to kick me out of the classroom. I've been here ever since, 'pending investigation.'"

"They're weasels! Didn't the investigation show you were innocent? Or is it still going on?"

"No, it ended some time ago. Every single child in my class -- where this 'crime' supposedly occurred -- denied I'd ever even mentioned prostitution. Only one child, who wasn't even in my class, for heaven's sake, backed up the claim I'd taught prostitution. Not surprisingly, his mother was a board member for this district, with close ties to Menendez. I've been here ever since. They can't fire me because I have tenure."

"Why'd they want to get you out of the classroom in the first place?"

"Because I'd started speaking up about the tracking system Menendez was using to place students in our gifted classes. It kept other immigrants out of our school, no matter how bright they were. Reverse discrimination, you know? That way the district could use our school exclusively for the boys and girls who were children of the local middle class. The middle class who controls the local Board of Ed. and Menendez."

"Are you kidding me?" David said so loudly that John looked over at them to make sure everything was okay.

"It's fine, John. David here is just getting upset – appropriately -- at our local Gestapo-like bureaucracy. Don't you know anything about Menendez, David?"

"Besides the fact that he's a slimy little creep? No. Only met him once, just now, upstairs."

"I was around when the School Chancellor nixed Menendez's first run for superintendent, back in the eighties. The Chancellor announced that Menendez was no leader in education, said he wasn't of high enough moral character for the position. He'd been caught for fraud when he submitted his application to run for a Democratic town leader position, a year or so before. A couple years later Menendez's sister and his brother-in-law, I think, became members of the district school board and suddenly – surprise, surprise -- Menendez himself became the superintendent. Then his sister got indicted for falsifying financial statements, but of course today she's a Democratic district leader. Now, given the district's Hispanic demographics, the community leaders are happy to have Menendez in the slot, even though our district's schools have about the lowest ranking in the state, let alone the city."

"Does all of this mean I'm screwed?" David asked, half jesting, half worried.

"Hate to say it, but could be. I never knew any of this to start off with, myself. I just loved going into my classroom and teaching every day. I found out the hard way, once I started opening my mouth. You know, ten years ago a grand jury discovered that in our district, of all the applications for para-professionals -- classroom aides and so forth -- only those with sponsors on the board were processed. I don't have a sponsor. I bet you don't either."

"Mrs. Jeffreys probably doesn't count, does she?"

"Mrs. Jeffreys?"

"The nurse at 232. She likes me. She could be my sponsor."

Anthony smiled. "If she changed her name to Gonzalez, yeah."

David pushed his chair back from the table and stood up, but didn't move anywhere.

"How come you never sued these guys?" he asked Anthony.

"Do you really think I'd win?" He laughed.

"How long have you been here anyway?"

"Five years."

"Jeez! How do you stay sane, doing nothing – sorry, you know what I mean – all day long?"

"I've been catching up on my reading." Anthony smiled and tapped the book in his hands. "And I've still got summers off. This time next year, I can retire with sixty percent." He looked directly up at David, more serious now. "At this point, I'm no longer proud."

"Well, I'm suing these bastards."

CHAPTER 6

David rang the doorbell and when Karen opened the door, he stuck his face right down into hers.

"Knock, knock!" he whispered, a big smile on his face.

"David! I didn't know you we're coming by."

"Well, I am."

"Come in. I don't know if I've got any food. Or soda. Wow, that's a great shirt you've got on. It's new?"

David's hands smoothed down the front of his blue and yellow Hawaiian shirt.

"Yeah. Nice, huh!"

"You might think about buying a size larger now, though. You know, so you can tuck it in."

She reached over and patted his round belly just above where the shirt rode up and exposed his hairy stomach.

"This is more comfortable," he said.

"Come, sit."

They went in and sat next to each other on the sofa.

"I hear you're working with dad on your legal stuff. That's nice, the two of you together," Karen said.

"Yeah. He knows a lot. I mean as a lawyer. I never knew that. He's good. We're gonna show these jerks who's boss."

Karen asked him about work and he filled her in on the charges against him, his removal from class and his transfer to the district office.

"And what ever happened with that gal you liked, Ms. Petrovitz?"

Karen asked him.

"Petrocelli? She's out."

"How come?"

"We can't do anything 'cause we work together. But we're best friends now. I gave her my Monopoly top hat token."

"Really?"

"Yeah. She likes me for all the things a woman should like me for. My mind. My values. My humor. My honor. All the important things. She wouldn't care if I didn't tuck my shirt in. That's the kind of woman she is. She knows what's right and what's wrong, and she fights for it. She knows the rules, too."

"She sounds nice."

"She is. She's the kind I think I'd still love even after we had an argument. She's the kind I could look into the eyes of and see her as the mother of my children. I'd know -- if something fatal happened to me tomorrow -- I'd know I'd still be comforted in those last five seconds of my life by the fact that she was the mother of my children. I always feel better after I've been around her for just five seconds. She's the kind of woman…"

"I get it, David. I get it. By the way, has dad told you about Michelle?"

"…except I can't see her anymore because I'm over in the District Office now and…"

"Did dad tell you about Michelle?"

"I don't think so."

"She's pregnant!"

"I've always wanted to be an uncle!" He went silent for a minute. "You and I will be the aunt and uncle who'll spoil that child to death, right?"

"Of course we will. What should I get Michelle now? You know, for a present? Diapers? Rattles? Breast pump? What? I don't know what to get her."

"Don't worry. It's a little early yet. She's not due til December."

"Well, that's still great!" David said. "What about you. When are you getting pregnant?"

"I'm not even married." She punched his shoulder.

"Oh, right. Of course." He punched her shoulder back, lightly, but she wasn't sure if he'd been kidding or not.

"Karen, I've got to go."

"Already? You sure? I can order some pizza if you want. Or hoagies. Chinese?"

"Nope. Gotta go. Dad wants me to research some old Board of Ed. suits. I'm going over to Touro."

"The law school?"

"Yup. Maybe I'll enroll there some day. Who knows? I like this law stuff. You know, it's lawyers who keep everybody doing what's right, you know, keep them obeying the rules."

"I guess that's one way to look at it," Karen said, following him to her front door.

"Of course it is," he said and was out the door and gone.

"You've got a problem," Vera Rubin said to David when he arrived the next morning.

"Of course, I do. Which one do you mean?"

"They've been asking me about everything you say and do, but I refused to tell them anything. I think they're going to try to get you out of here."

"Wait a minute. Who's 'they'?"

"You know. Mrs. Crawford, Menendez's secretary, and the Deputy Superintendent's right hand man, Borman. He's our 'Director of Operations.' For some reason, they left the 'Covert' out of his title. Crawford came down yesterday and wanted to know what you've been saying to me. Borman came by afterward and searched the computer you work on to see if you'd written up anything about what's going on. He couldn't find anything."

"There's nothing to find. Do they think I'm stupid enough to leave anything for them on one of their own computers?"

"Well, Crawford said they're probably going to get you out of here and put you someplace where they can keep an eye on you…seeing I wasn't going to tell them anything."

"Thank you, Vera."

"That's the least I could do, but watch yourself. They're going to have to make some excuse to get you transferred. I know. I've seen this sort of thing before, where I came from."

"The Bronx?"

"No, I live in the Bronx. I came from Russia. Kiev. When it was still the Soviet Union. This guy Borman is like a little KGB agent, I'll tell you. Same sneaky eyes and same dark shadow hanging over him. Scary man."

"He works for the Deputy Superintendent? I don't know him. Yet."

"Yeah, for Partridge. Menendez promoted him from being an assistant principal over on the west side. He's the Hearing Officer for grievances, too. That way they can keep control over who's being targeted to quit and who they want to favor. Anyway, sounds like he's out to get you. Maybe because you're Jewish, huh?"

"I don't think being Jewish has anything to do with it. It's 'cause I won't shut up."

"Yeah, but you don't see any other Jews working here in the district, do you?"

"No, I don't, but frankly, Vera, most Jews my age are on their way to becoming doctors, lawyers or dentists, not working as teachers in inner city schools."

"See. What'd I tell you? No Jews here. Except you, of course. Oh. By the way. Some woman came by and dropped something off for you. I forget her name."

Vera walked over to her desk, picked up a business envelope and handed it to David.

"It's from Lisa, my union rep. My ex-union rep."

He undid the clasp, pulled out a single page letter typed on official school stationery and read through it quickly.

"I can't believe it. Listen to this. It's from Dr. Harrison, my principal. 'Dear Mr. Weintraub. As per the Superintendent's request, you are to report to his office immediately. Thank you for your attention to this matter.' She knew she had to provide me with a written order, but here she's weaseling out of any responsibility for anything. See. She's laying it all on Menendez. You know, my new union rep here has been telling me I don't need any written letters from anyone about my transfer. She must be in cahoots with these guys, too, huh?"

"Nothing would surprise me about this place. It's a bureaucracy gone mad. Just like the Soviet Union."

Two days later David was sitting across and down from Vera, in front of his computer, reading the newest *Sports Illustrated*. He'd stretched his legs up and out to his right and he had his feet crossed, propped up on the table by the computer next to him.

Borman came into the computer room and walked directly over to David.

"Weintraub!" He yelled. "Get your feet off that table! You could bash in one of our computers with your feet like that. They're worth a lot of money, you know. Get your stuff and come with me. Now."

While David put his feet down and stuffed his magazine into his briefcase, Borman grabbed a piece of paper from a ream next to one of the printers, wrote on it and folded it once.

"Come on," he said and led David out of the room, up the stairs and down the hall into Menendez's office. He handed Mrs. Crawford the folded piece of paper. David wondered, by the calm look on her face, maybe she'd been expecting Borman.

She took a long time reading the piece of paper even though David could see it only had one short line written on it. She kept twisting her thumb and forefinger around one short strand of her hair from the side of her pixie cut while she went over and over the note.

"Thank you, Mr. Borman," she said after she had set the paper down carefully on her desk. "Mr. Weintraub, I'm going to reassign you to another area. I don't think you're showing the respect necessary for the computer equipment we have. It's quite valuable, you know."

"I do know that, but I have found, so far in my life, that I have complete control of my feet, Mrs. Crawford. I don't think there was any great danger of my foot suddenly destroying the computer in front of me."

"Mr. Borman, can you please escort Mr. Weintraub down to that seat in the hallway outside the personnel office? Thank you."

"Follow me," Borman said to David.

"Just a second," David said and walked over and sat down on the couch across from Mrs. Crawford's desk. He pulled his yellow pad out of his briefcase and started writing. He noticed the surprised, and then angry look Borman gave Menendez's secretary as he wrote.

"Okay. I'm ready. Let's go," David said, standing and smiling after he slid his pad back into his briefcase.

Borman led David up two flights of stairs to the third floor and down a main hall before he turned into a short, narrow hallway on the left which had an entrance to the personnel office on one side and a men's room door on the other. There was a folding metal chair at the end in front of two wall lockers. The wooden floor in front of the chair was warped from moisture and deep in dust.

"You can use that chair for the moment," Borman said.

"No, I can't. You know I have the right to be assigned to a room, not a hallway, while I'm on administrative leave over here. Says so in the regulations. If you want to assign me to Personnel, you'll have to seat me in their office itself."

David pointed to the door to his left as he pulled his yellow pad out of his briefcase.

"Wait here," Borman said, turned and walked quickly away.

Ten minutes later he returned.

"You're being assigned to the Early Childhood department. Second floor. Follow me."

Menendez had changed his mind, David realized. He probably didn't want him anywhere near the personnel office.

"You can have Mrs. Wilson's desk," a squat bodied woman with straight, graying hair said to David after Borman had left him in the Early Childhood office. "She's the department head, but she's on vacation this month. Of course, she's retiring at the end of the year so she's always kind of on vacation these days. I'm Miriam Smith, her assistant. You're Weintraub, right?"

"David. Yes."

"What are you're here at the district offices for? Some court case, I heard."

"No court case. Just charges. But they'll be thrown out any day now," David said to her as nonchalantly as he could while he set his briefcase down on Mrs. Wilson's desk and pulled out his yellow pad.

"What's that for?" Mrs. Smith asked. She stood by the doorway of the small office, eyeing David.

"In case I have to write anything down. You know, evidence," David told her. He was pretty sure Miriam Smith would be reporting back to those in the main office everything he was doing or saying so he thought he would put her on guard immediately by taking his pad out.

"Well, there's not going to be anything I say to you that you'll need to write down," she said and walked over to her desk on the other side of the little room and sat down behind it, still eyeballing David. "They took you out of the computer room, huh?"

This woman is going to be pumping me for as much information as she can, David thought, and reporting it back to the brass downstairs. That's it! That's perfect! I can use her to pass on exactly what I want Menendez to hear. They want mind games? I'll give them mind games.

"You know," David said, "they kicked me out of Vera Rubin's office for – can you believe it – putting my feet on the table, but that's just one more thing they're going to have to account for when I take them to court. They won't have a chance."

"You're taking them to court?"

"I'm certainly thinking about it. Do you know how much evidence I already have, written down right here?" David patted the yellow pad on the desk in front of him. "This is the fourth pad I've filled out."

He gave her a practiced smile from across the room.

"Now, here's something else," he continued and reached into his briefcase and pulled out the envelope with Dr. Harrison's letter which he'd gotten from Ms. Petrocelli. "See this? More evidence. It's a letter from my principal -- you know, Dr. Harrison – saying I'm to report to the district offices, but she gives absolutely no reason why I'm to do so. Can you believe how stupid these people are?"

"Alright, Mr. Weintraub. I've got work to do now," Miriam said and picked up a folder from the edge of her desk. She opened it up and leaned closely over it, peering intently at the paperwork in it.

David took out his *Sports Illustrated* from his briefcase and started reading about the World Series chances for the Yankees this season.

The next morning, when David arrived, Miriam motioned him over to her desk.

"This is for you, Mr. Weintraub," she said and handed him an envelope with the District Office title and address printed on it.

David took it over to his desk, sat down and opened it. On official District Office letterhead it read,

You have been assigned to the district office pending the outcome of a police investigation concerning allegations that have been lodged against you. Thank you for your cooperation in this matter.
Sincerely, Ramon Menendez, District Superintendent.

That was fast, David thought.

He stuffed the letter back into the envelope and put it in his briefcase. He knew Miriam was still watching him and he kept a serious expression on his face, but inside he was thrilled. This was the written evidence he needed. He loved it! Now, as soon as the police investigation was concluded and the charges were thrown out – as he was confident they would be, based on what his lawyer had told him – there would be no reason for him to be held at the district office and he could return to teaching his class back at P.S. 232.

"You know, Mrs. Smith," David called out across the room, "it seems to me that justice always prevails in the end. The little guy has rights and there are laws and rules to protect him so no one can take advantage of him. It's a good country we live in, don't you think?"

"I really don't know. I guess so," she said without looking up from the paperwork she had on the desk in front of her. "Why don't you run down to the staff cafeteria and hang out for awhile. I really don't have anything for you to do here. There's an old sofa in the back of the room there. I've seen some other teachers napping on it. Nobody cares."

"This is like an endless sensory deprivation experiment," David said to Vera Rubin several weeks later. He'd snuck into her office after lunch to tell her the latest and catch up on any news she might have for him. Anthony Nelson gave David's presence a quick acknowledgement with one finger in the air while he kept on reading his novel at the back of the room.

"Nobody has anything for me to do," David said. "They're trying to wear me down with inertia. Some days it feels like it's working. I hate having nothing to do. You know, I've started staying up til three in the morning, then I drag myself in here and punch the clock, then sleep on the cafeteria sofa til lunchtime. I punch out, go down to the bodega for lunch, come back, punch in and do crossword puzzles, read, write, until I punch out at the end of the day. Mindless. A weaker person would have gone nuts by now."

"Sounds like a Siberian internment camp to me," Vera said.

"I knew you'd understand," David said.

They chatted for awhile and then David peeked out the door into the hallway, saw it was empty and started walking down toward the stairwell. Half way down the hall David spotted a math project display board for square roots which had somehow fallen onto the floor from a table by the wall that had a number of other small posters on it displaying various math formulas and principles. David picked up the one that had fallen on the floor, wiped it off with his sleeve and placed it back on the table.

"What the hell are you doing with my exhibit?" David heard someone behind him yell. He turned and saw Mr. Rome, the overseer of the district's mathematics departments, barreling down on him from the doorway Rome had just come out of.

"Calm down," David said. "This piece fell on the floor. I'm just putting it back,"

"You're putting it down in completely the wrong place. Can't you tell where it's supposed to go?" Rome moved the square root placard down two feet to the left on the table. "There. That's where it goes. You've got a lot of gall messing around with that. You're the guy who got kicked out of 232, right?"

David swatted the poster off the table and back down onto the floor.

Rome clenched his fists and took a step toward David. He was a few inches shorter than David, but heavy set and barrel-chested. David looked down into his red face.

"You know," David said, "I saw in the morning paper last week that there's been a double digit drop, district wide, in mathematics proficiency tests this last year. Congratulations on the fine job you've been doing, sir. You must be very proud."

Rome raised his fists in front of him and pushed one into David's lower chest.

"Why don't you just come outside with me, youngster?" he said, his face even redder than it had been.

David stood still and stared at him. Yep, humor is an effective tool, David thought, for someone in my position to keep his spirits up. Ghandi as a jokester. MLK with a flashy punch line. I love it.

Rome started pushing against David's chest and David began pushing back.

"Hold it! Hold it, you two!"

Dr. Menendez had just come into the hallway from the rear stairwell and was now striding toward David and Rome.

"That's enough of that! Rome, what do you think you're doing? Back to your office! Weintraub, where are you supposed to be?"

"Sofa in the cafeteria, sir," David said.

"Well, get there," Menendez said.

Two days later David's lawyer called him at home in the evening to tell him that the police had completed their investigation and the charges had been dropped altogether.

"Those guys really don't like you, do they?" his lawyer said. "Detective Sweeney told me, off the record, that he thought the whole thing was completely contrived. They just wanted you out of there."

"They still do," David said.

The next morning he went to Menendez's office as soon as he had punched in.

"The police have dropped the charges," David said to Mrs. Crawford. "Tell the superintendent I'm ready to go back to my classroom."

"Have a seat, Mr. Weintraub, while I talk to Dr. Menendez."

"I'll stand. I'm ready to go back to P.S. 232, Mrs. Crawford. Right now," David said and folded his arms across his chest, back arched, still standing right in front of her desk.

"Suit yourself," she said, stood and went back into Menendez's office.

In several minutes Menendez came out, Mrs. Crawford behind him.

"Mr. Weintraub, I appreciate your eagerness to return to teaching, but I'm afraid you can't do that yet. Even though the police have cleared you, the downtown Board of Ed. Office hasn't finished their investigation of the matter yet."

"That's ridiculous. The police cleared me. I'll file a grievance."

"It'll be thrown out, Mr. Weintraub. I would have thought you -- of all people -- would know that. The Board of Ed. is perfectly within their rights to conduct their own investigation before they allow you to return to having any interaction with students."

David stood there in silence, running through his mind what he should do next.

"There's also this matter," Menendez said and handed David a manila envelope. "This is Dr. Harrison's last evaluation of you as a teacher. She's given you a "U" -- unsatisfactory – I'm afraid."

David ripped the tab off the end of the envelope and it fell to the floor as he pulled out the evaluation form. He scanned it over quickly. Eighteen out of twenty-three categories were marked "unsatisfactory," even "housekeeping and appearance of room." At the bottom Harrison had recommended denying David certification, thereby preventing him from working anywhere else in the New York City school system.

"This, this, I can file a grievance on," David said.

"That, you can," Menendez said and returned to his office.

David turned and left, but halfway down the hallway he realized he'd need to get the grievance forms from Mrs. Crawford because he knew Mrs. Bradshaw, the district union rep, was on six week leave after just having given birth.

He turned, walked back down the hall, opened the superintendent's front office door without knocking and stopped in his tracks.

Dr. Harrison was just leaving Menendez's office.

"Oh, hello, David," she said and her fingers went immediately to her beads as she whisked by him on her way out through the office door he was still holding open.

David immediately pulled his yellow pad out and started writing.

"Mr. Weintraub, you'll have to do that somewhere else," Mrs. Crawford said to him and came around from behind her desk to push him by his shoulder out the door.

"I need some grievance forms before I leave, Mrs. Crawford."

She stopped, glared at David and went back to her desk and found two grievance forms for him. She stood next to her desk scowling and holding them out in the air in front of her.

He walked over and took them and slid them into his briefcase.

"I must say, Mr. Weintraub, you really are a piece of work, aren't you," she said.

"That I am," he said and threw his best smile ever at her.

Later that morning, as David filled out the grievance forms for Harrison's unfair evaluation while slouched down on the sofa in the staff cafeteria, one foot up on the cushion, Borman came into the room and walked over to David.

"Get off that sofa, Weintraub. This isn't a yoga class."

"I've got every right to sit, or even sleep, here. You bureaucrats do it all the time," David said.

"Look at this," Borman said pointing at the edge of the cushion. "It's filthy where your foot is."

David took his foot off the cushion.

Borman hesitated, then spoke.

"I want you to go get that cushion cleaned off. Take it down to maintenance. Right now."

"You'll have to put that in writing, sir." David said.

"Here. Give me that," Borman said. He reached down and took the yellow pad from the other cushion on the sofa where David had put it.

Borman shuffled down through all the pages that had writing on them until he found the first blank page. He leaned over and rested the pad on his thigh while he wrote the order for David to get the cushion cleaned. He dated and signed it.

"See. Look at this," Borman said to one of the two young men sitting together nearby at one of the cafeteria tables. "See this. Evidence. Right here. An order to get the cushion cleaned."

He brandished the yellow pad high in the air and started to turn to leave, pad still in hand.

"Give me that," David yelled, stood and yanked the pad out of Borman's hand as he started to walk away.

"Give that back to me!" Borman yelled. "That order's my evidence." He reached out and pulled at the pad.

"It's my pad," David yelled and pulled back.

"It's my order!"

"It's my pad!"

David grabbed the pad away from Borman and ripped off the page with his order on it, crumpled it up and stuffed it down the front of his pants.

"Come and get it," he said, calm again, and smiling.

Borman spun on his heel and left the room.

The two young men sitting at the nearby table started clapping. Three women, sitting together at the table in the far corner of the room, stared at David, unsure what had just happened.

"Hey!" the young man nearest David called over to him. "Aren't you that guy my buddy over at 232 told me about who did that toothpick trick for your class? You know, like in *Rain Man*." He picked up a small glass jar of toothpicks from the cluster of salt and pepper shakers, ketchup and mustard bottles in the center of his table. He waved the little jar in front of him. "Was he just bustin' on me or can you really do that?"

"Dump it out," David said as he walked to over to the table.

The three women rose from their chairs and hurried over to the table behind the two young men. The one with the toothpick jar, in his early twenties with a clean, but wrinkled blue shirt, heavily moussed black hair and a wisp of a beard tracing his jaw line, waited for them to reach the table before he dumped the toothpicks out on the shiny white surface of the table.

"Eighty-nine," David said without hesitation.

The two men started counting the toothpicks.

"Forty-three," the one said when he'd finished.

"Forty-six," the other in the blue shirt said. "That's frigging amazing! Do another one."

He pointed at the next table over and one of the women went and got the toothpick jar from it and brought it back to him. He dumped out the toothpicks.

"Seventy-one," David said.

"What are you, some kind of genius?" the man in the blue shirt said after the two of them had counted out the toothpicks. There were seventy-one.

One of the other women went and got the toothpick jar from the next table over and David called out the number of toothpicks on the table after she'd emptied the glass jar. He was off by one.

85

"Here, let's try it again," the woman said and went and brought back the last toothpick jar from the farthest table where the women had been sitting.

The man in the blue shirt dumped it out in front of him.

"Eighty-two," David said.

The two men counted, looked at each other and shook their heads.

"Right on!" the blue shirt said. He held up his hand in the air and David high-fived it. "How the hell do you do that?"

"I don't know," David said. "I really don't. I just do it."

They all applauded and David walked back over to the sofa, eased himself down into it, pulled out his yellow pad, stretched, and lifted both his feet up onto the cushion.

CHAPTER 7

David knew by the end of April that he would be able to hold out until the last day of school in June.

He had been letting everyone he met in the school know that he was going to sue, and it seemed that his PR campaign was paying off. There had been no more harassment since the incident with Borman in the district cafeteria. David's grievance of Dr. Harrison's Unsatisfactory evaluation had not been accepted altogether, but instead of eighteen unsatisfactory categories, it now only contained six, not enough to disqualify David from being employed anywhere else in the New York City school system.

Menendez was still stalling on putting David back into the classroom, but David knew the longer he kept David from teaching because of the bogus "downtown running its own investigation" ploy, the worse it would look for these "weasels." In the long run, his lawsuit would benefit.

David and his father had been working together Saturday mornings formatting his harassment suit, and his father had begun research on filing a civil rights violation as well. David's case could be exemplary, he thought, because of the school officials' suppression of David's First Amendment rights, and it could turn out to be a precedent setting case that would protect any employee in the future -- particularly those in the government or in large organizations -- from the vindictiveness David had been subjected to.

David's biggest challenge was keeping himself busy and motivated throughout the endless tedium of day after day on the cafeteria sofa. Miriam Smith had given up – or had been told to give up -- trying to keep him busy and had suggested he just stay in the cafeteria and out of her hair. He kept to his schedule of arriving tired, snoozing on the sofa until late morning, punching out for lunch and returning and trying to keep himself entertained for the remainder of the school day.

He could keep himself happy with a turkey hoagie, sautéed peppers and a thirty-two ounce Cherry Cola at the local bodega as many days of the week as he wanted, and he realized if every two weeks he took a sick day from the ten he had left, he'd feel rejuvenated enough from his day off to carry on a while longer. He spent more and more of his days off in the Touro law library, partially to help out his dad with the law case, partially because he had begun to feel at home there.

Finally, with nothing else to do and to keep himself busy so he wouldn't "lose his mind," as he had told Michelle, during the last two weeks of May he decided to rewrite the Bible, word for word, Old Testament and New -- the way he felt it should have been written in the first place. He began his foreword with:

"The root of most conservatism and most world evil comes from religious bibles. Discredit the validity and veracity of the bible and the world becomes a much more beautiful place. For those who claim that the bible is not to be taken literally or is merely allegories, you are excused. For those who take the bible literally or as God's undeniable word, you are not excused."

David had always particularly objected to God's saying "I will greatly increase your pains in childbearing; with pain you will give birth to children" and that divine threat angered him even more now that Michelle was pregnant. He also hated God's rule of "Do not wear clothing woven of these two kinds of material…" and as he had started off merely rewriting these phrases to his liking, he had begun to get more and more carried away and he went ahead and rewrote everything else, as well, the way he thought it should be, on a stack of new yellow legal pads that he now carried into the cafeteria with him every day.

He began writing political opinion, too, late into the night on his home computer and he soon became known as "davefromqueens" on his own daily blog that he'd created. He wrote of his concern that the Supreme Court Justices had become too conservative and were undermining the Constitution, he offered nine sure fire talking points for any liberal candidate to easily lord it over conservative or moderate opponents, and he sometimes played with political poetry to entertain his readers and express his views.

He became especially proud of one poem he wrote and he posted it on several different blogs besides his own. He titled it "Conservative Republicans, Filthy Pigs, They Undermine America" and it could be sung to the tune of "Yankee Doodle Dandy."

Killing millions just for oil, funding dictators who torture and boil
Allowing their Pearl Harbor on American soil, a plot they ignored and did not foil.
Salmonella in your food, sixty bucks for a barrel of crude,
protecting wrongdoers from being sued, higher interest rates you're getting screwed

Conservative Republicans, Filthy Pigs, they undermine America.

Gas prices at record high, more pollutants in your sky
Mercury in your water supply, they don't care if you live or die.
Cutting funding in your schools, dummy downed tests written for fools,
Void of ethics, can't play by the rules, Neal Horsley's first girlfriend was a mule.

Conservative Republicans, Filthy Pigs, they undermine America.

He started going to political rallies for Democrats campaigning in local elections in Connecticut, New Jersey and New York, and he became known for wearing a rubber caricature mask of George Bush, the younger. At one rally and parade in Newtown, Connecticut, he broke free from the crowd, crossing over the parade barriers and ran up right next to Senator Joe Lieberman, marching along with the local candidate. He had on his Bush mask and his white golf shirt rode high on his stomach over his black Bermuda shorts. The first expression on the senator's face suggested he really didn't know what to make of David, or even if he might be dangerous, but Lieberman finally smiled once at the hulking David and then quickened his pace to catch back up to the candidate.

Local TV stations loved playing the footage of David's large frame towering over the trim Lieberman, and local newspapers ran photos and articles of the event for the next several days.

The now locally renowned "davefromqueens" claimed afterward on his blog that he had achieved his prescribed fifteen minutes of fame, and suddenly David had an audience of equally impassioned liberals championing "the little guy" as much as David did. He loved it.

He also spent more and more time with his sister Michelle now that she was close to giving birth and now that Karen had become far busier with college. Michelle would tell him she was "nesting" in preparation for the arrival of the baby, and David started cleaning and tidying up his own apartment so that he could tell her he was now nesting, too, right along with her. He couldn't wait to be an uncle.

Occasionally David would sneak back over to P.S. 232 and meet with Lisa Petrocelli. They played up their cloak and dagger routines by his slinking down the hallway outside her office, squeezing quickly past her door, locking it behind him, and then the two of them whispered back and forth to each other their news as they sat, head to head, Scarlet and Plum, at her desk.

One day Lisa told David she heard that Miranda Gonzalez's mother had threatened to hire a lawyer because her daughter wasn't learning anything with "all those other people in there."

"Your class has turned into a zoo," Lisa told him. "Schneider's new secretary told me one day she walked by your old room, heard all sorts of noise, peeked in saw children climbing on the desks and running chaotically around the room. Half your kids have been removed from your class and placed in other classes. Schneider's gone through twelve different teachers for your class since you left."

"I wonder if any of them have been rated 'Unsatisfactory,'" David said. "You know the worst thing about all of this, though?"

"What?"

"These kids won't be able to make up for what they've lost this half year. I know Miranda will be able to pull through anything. Maybe even Bobby Martinez, too. But the others are just doomed. In school and in life. At least they'd had half a chance there for awhile."

"I know. Thank God you're taking these guys – sorry, these weasels, -- to court. Want to hear something funny, though? I heard that after Schneider's last write up of you got rejected by the grievance officer, Schneider told him 'I guess I just don't document as well as Weintraub.' Isn't that a hoot?"

"Hoots are what we're going for, Lisa. Hoots and justice."

In early June David was on his way to the bodega for his lunch when he saw his ex-student Julio Garcia walking toward him with a man dressed in a worn green work shirt and matching work pants, perhaps his father, David guessed. Julio had a puffy white bandage taped across his left eye.

David squatted down in front of the boy and touched the edge of the bandage.

"Julio, what happened?" David asked him.

The boy hung his head.

"I'm Julio's father," the man said. "There's a wild kid at school, Jesus – I don't know if you know him or not. He stabbed Julio in the eye with a pencil." He placed a calloused hand on the side of his son's face. "We had to take him to the emergency room. He got fifteen stitches. We don't know what'll happen to his eye."

"I am so sorry," David said. "Yes, I do know Jesus. He should have been removed from school months, maybe years ago."

"I'm going to the district office right now to take Julio out of 232. I had to take the day off from work 'cause his mother couldn't. Something has to be done."

"You're doing the right thing, Mr. Garcia. I am so sorry."

"You're Julio's old teacher, aren't you? Why did they take you out of there?"

"Because I was too good," David said. He patted Julio on the shoulder, shook Mr. Garcia's hand and walked quickly away toward the bodega.

This is why people go postal, David thought. This, this, is exactly what's wrong with the world. One, two, three, four, five six seven.

Three weeks later David got up with a smile on his face, one he'd never practiced. Today was his next to last day at school. He'd made it.

"No more weasels, no more crooks, no more Borman's dirty looks," David sang to himself as he watched out the train window as the clean suburban sprawl of Queens turned into the dirty brownstones and dusty tenements of Brooklyn.

As he walked from the station to the district office, the June sun felt warm on his forehead, even so early in the morning, and the ten year old gangbangers he passed on the corner, all sharing a cigarette, looked happier to David than usual. They'd made the sunny corner their own this morning instead of huddling back in the shadowy tenement doorways.

Today was going to be a great day, David thought. He'd considered calling out that morning, to use up his last sick day, but he'd decided he'd rather enjoy his quiet triumph by happily walking up and down the district office halls and showing them he'd outlasted them all in this six month battle of wills.

He stopped in the bodega and bought himself a thirty-two ounce Cherry Cola to celebrate the day and he sipped it as he walked the rest of the way to the district offices humming Alice Cooper's "School's Out for the Summer."

"Good morning, beautiful," David called out to Vera as he stuck his head in through the computer room doorway.

"David, you've just about made it! Only one day to go," she said.

In the back of the room Anthony looked up from his book, held his thumb high in the air and jerked it emphatically at David.

"Here's a little morning treat for you two," David said and handed her the box of four fresh donuts he'd picked up for them. "You know, to celebrate."

"Thank you," she said and looked into the box. "There's four. Do you want one?"

"Well, I might."

After they'd finished the donuts – David accepting both extra Boston Cremes, his favorite, after Vera and Anthony had each eaten their one – David made his way upstairs to the cafeteria and plopped down onto the sofa. He was hoping Lisa might sneak by for a minute to say hello, but only a few other district staff came by for a mid-morning coffee and to chit-chat with David while he worked on the daily *Times* crossword and some math puzzles from the Sudoku paperback he carried with him.

Just before noon he went and punched out and made his way back over to the bodega for lunch. As he neared the front door under the faded green awning of the shop, he heard someone yelling behind him. He turned and saw Ms. Fontagne with one of the school aides and two children in tow.

"You frigging hit me!" Ms. Fontagne yelled at David.

"What are you talking about? Are you nuts?" David yelled back.

"Well, you hit me with a pencil!"

David had fended off other attempts at the district office to bait him into doing something stupid -- like Mr. Rome challenging him to fight -- and he thought Ms. Fontagne had probably been put up to do something similar. He smirked at having recognized her ploy, but he wasn't going to fall for that trap. He turned and went into the bodega to order his lunch.

When David came out, paper bag and drink in hand, his eyes adjusting to the June sun after the shadowy interior of the store, he saw Ms. Fontagne again, now standing on the sidewalk near the corner, the aide and the two children still with her. She began yelling at David. A few passersby looked at her, but most walked past her, ignoring her tirade. To them she was just one more crazy person on the street.

Fontagne ploy was like a tricky chess game challenge, David thought, this time from the King's hippie bishop. He decided his rebuttal would be to step quickly off the curb and cross the street. He did, pausing once in the middle to let a speeding cab go by before continuing to walk back to the district office without once looking back at Fontagne.

"Gambit declined. Score one more for Ghandi," David said under his breath and took a long sip of his Cherry Cola as he walked along the sidewalk, smiling at the people he passed even though they walked quickly by, ignoring him.

Back at the district office he punched his time card, went to the cafeteria and sat at the nearest table to write down on his yellow pad everything that had just happened. Then he went over and settled into the sofa to continue his puzzles and napping for the afternoon.

Forty-five minutes later Mr. Schneider walked through the cafeteria door. David sat straight up. He hadn't seen Schneider for months.

"Mr. Weintraub, you have visitors," Schneider said and stepped to his left, holding the door open behind him.

Two uniformed New York City policemen walked in. David didn't recognize either of them. Maybe they weren't from the local precinct.

Behind them was Freddie Donnelly, the 232 school safety and security guard who David had said hello to as he arrived at school every morning. Ms. Fontagne came in last and stood to their right.

David stood up from the sofa to face them all.

The older policemen, who had a string of gold stripes on his sleeve, asked David, "Do you know why we're here?"

"I have no idea, but I could probably make a pretty good guess," he said, eyeing Ms. Fontagne.

"There's been an accusation made," the policeman said and turned to his right and looked at Ms. Fontagne.

"Yes," she said and pointed to David with a scarlet fingernail. "He's the one. He's the one who stabbed me. He stabbed me and said, 'Oops. Now you know what it feels like to be stabbed in the back.' That's him."

"This woman is delusional, officer," David said. "Who reported this?"

"I'm not sure who called in the 911," the officer said. "Was that you, Mr. Schneider?"

"No, Dr. Harrison was the one who informed me, but I thought she said 911 had already been called. Maybe by Officer Donnelly?" Schneider looked over at the security guard.

"No, sir. I was told by you that 911 had been called when you had me talk to Ms. Fontagne. Perhaps she'd already called 911."

"No," Ms. Fontagne said. "I reported what happened to Dr. Harrison when I came back from lunch and she said 911 should be called and then she got Mr. Schneider. I never called 911. I just told what happened."

"Alright, alright, all of you," the lead officer said. "911 was called, somehow, and we drove over to the school and then we all waked over here. 'Assault with a weapon' is the charge, Mr. Weintraub."

"I don't know what you are talking about," David said. "What 'weapon'?"

"A pencil," the officer said.

"A pencil?!" David said and looked over at Schneider as if for his agreement that the charge was ridiculous. Schneider stood with his hands clasped in front of him, not moving, not saying anything, but David thought he could see the pleasure in his eyes.

"Ms. Fontagne," the senior policeman said, "you can fill out the complaint now, if you would." He nodded to the other policeman, who handed Ms. Fontagne a single form. "Officer Donnelly, you can be the signing officer here and you can make the arrest."

Freddie stepped forward and tried to contain the broad smile that had appeared on his face when he heard he would be the arresting officer.

Ms. Fontagne took the paper over to the nearest cafeteria table and leaned over it as she started to fill the form out with a pen she had pulled from her hemp shoulder bag. When she bent over, the head of the green and blue peacock tattoo stared up at the ceiling from above the short collar of her dress. Officer Donnelly stood behind her and stared down at the brightly colorful bird.

No one spoke while Fontagne filled out the form. When she was done, she straightened up, offered Donnelly her pen and he leaned forward and wrote out his signature and the date. He handed the form to the younger officer.

"Mr. Schneider, I think we're done here," the senior officer said. "Here's my card if you need to reach me."

Schneider stepped forward to take the blue and gold card from the officer's hand.

"I'll walk you back to the school, if you'd like," Schneider said to Ms. Fontagne. The two officers stepped aside to let them exit before following them out the door.

Donnelly turned to David.

"I'll have to frisk you, Mr. Weintraub."

"What? To make sure I don't have any more pencils on me?"

Donnelly stepped up close to David, who was almost a foot taller than he, and patted down his sides and legs before turning him around and going down his back and both his legs again with his fluttering hands. After he'd checked both of David's ankles, he stood, gently pulled David's hands together behind his back and snapped them together with the handcuffs he'd pulled from his belt.

"Isn't anybody going to ask *me* what happened?" David asked, more to the empty cafeteria in front of him than to Donnelly himself.

"I guess not," Donnelly said and led David out of the room.

David stumbled every few feet as he made his way down the hallway. His body felt like it was being pulled out of whack with his hands bound behind him and with Donnelly's unconfident guiding of him down the hall.

At the top of the stairs they ran into two of the women who David had performed the toothpick trick for in the cafeteria, coming back from a late lunch. The women stepped aside, their backs pressed against the smooth wall of the staircase, to let David and Donnelly pass slowly and awkwardly by them and go step by step down the stairwell. David felt ashamed that the two women had to see him in handcuffs. He hoped he wouldn't cry.

As the two police officers came out of Menendez's office downstairs, they met up with David and Freddie in the main hall and the four of them walked together to the front entrance. By this time several staff had come to the doors of their office and stuck their heads out to watch the foursome exit the building.

David made his way carefully down the thick granite steps of the building to the police car parked in front in the no parking zone. Of course, David said to himself. These guys can break any of the rules they want. Across the street an unshaven man elbowed the man sitting next to him on the stoop of a dilapidated brownstone. He pointed at David, said something to his pal and they both laughed.

This is the worst day of my life, David thought

The NYPD officers got in the front of the squad car, but Donnelly had to work hard to help David fold himself up enough, hands still locked together behind him, to get in through the back door of the car and down onto the back seat. David had to keep leaning forward so he wouldn't squash his hands against the back of the seat, and he bent his neck forward to keep the top of his head from pressing against the car's padded headliner. His whole body hurt.

"Sorry about all this, Mr. Weintraub," Donnelly said as he slid into the seat next to David.

At least no one's read me my Miranda rights yet, David realized, and he wished he had his yellow pad with him to write that injustice down. He was worried he might forget it. Everything had been happening way too fast for him since the first startling moment when Schneider had walked into the cafeteria. One, two, three, four, five, six, seven, he repeated to himself as the black and white pulled away from the curb.

As the car made its way through Brooklyn mid-day traffic, horns peeping, bus exhausts noisily whooshing out their diesel fumes against the sides of passing cars, David suddenly wondered what Ghandi would do in this circumstance. The answer was immediate.

He'd keep his mouth shut.

Okay, that's my strategy too, David thought, and he knew it would not be a hard one for him to carry out. He was too scared, really, to talk. Maybe the first time that had ever happened. A lot of people he could think of would probably have been happy not to have to listen to him.

They pulled up in front of the 83rd Precinct, a hundred year old brick building with a rounded tower on the top over the front corner. It gave the structure the appearance of a medieval jail. Donnelly climbed out his door and came around the car to help David work himself painfully up and out of the back seat. The two officers had already walked up the long flight of steps toward the heavy wooden doors of the entrance.

David struggled to climb the cement steps, the toes of his cordovans catching on every other rise, Donnelly bracing himself against David's falling forward. Freddie kept pressing the metal of the handcuffs against the soft skin of David's wrists every time he lunged forward. Their foreheads were dripping with sweat by the time they reached the top step, and although David was frightened of all that was going on, he was snapping angrily at Donnelly.

"Watch what you're doing. You're hurting me," David repeated all the way up the steps.

Inside, Donnelly guided David over to the watch officer behind the glass partition and waited with David until another officer came out and took David through the door at the far end of the partition. Donnelly followed him and then turned into a break room, sat down with a couple other cops with thick paper cups of coffee from a vending machine.

As David was being led back to an older officer sitting at a desk at the end of the hallway, he overheard Freddie begin telling the cops sitting at the table how he'd just made his first arrest.

"You can take his cuffs off, Frank," the officer at the desk said to the cop still holding on to David's upper arm as the two of them walked up. He took a key from his pocket, undid David's handcuffs and took them with him back to the front of the precinct.

"Wallet, keys, watch, valuables, shoe laces. Put 'em all in here," the officer said and held out a large manila envelope, spreading it open with his liver-spotted hands for David to drop everything into.

"Shoelaces?" David asked.

"Don't want you hanging yourself in the cell back there."

"That isn't happening," David said.

"That's right. Not if we have your shoelaces up here, it isn't."

"Innocent men don't hang themselves, officer."

The old cop eyed David suspiciously.

"Maybe not," he said.

Once David had filled the envelope, the officer eased himself slowly out of his creaking swivel chair and motioned for David to follow him over to the counter against the far wall. He picked up a little roller and a thin black bottle, squirted some ink onto the rubber pad and then fitted a thick paper form into the metal brackets attached to the counter.

"Fingerprint time," he said and reached out for David's hand after he'd rolled the ink across the pad. "Index finger, left hand first."

David kept getting confused about which finger he was supposed to hold out next as the officer started going through all ten, holding each down on the pad before pushing it into the labeled boxes on the form.

"Jesus Christ. You've screwed this all up," he said after David's left pinky finger jerked and made a long smear of black ink across the form. David's forehead was covered again by shiny beads of sweat.

The officer ripped the form out from the brackets and slid another one in.

"Let's try this one more time," the man muttered. "You nervous or something?"

"Something," David said quietly.

When he'd finished imprinting the second form, he gave David an alcohol soaked cloth to clean his fingertips with and then led him through a door and down a corridor with barred cells on both sides. He stopped at the last one on the right, took out a key and opened the heavy door.

"Your home for the next coupla hours," he said and tugged at David's arm to lead him into the cell before swinging the iron-bar door shut behind him. The loud clanging of the latch fastening itself echoed down the hallway and an older man who was sleeping up against the left wall inside the cell moved his shoulders and torso a bit, but did not wake up.

A young Latino boy in a black tee shirt and black jeans sat on the metal bench that was attached to the other wall, his back arched against the concrete blocks behind him, his hands stuffed deep into his pants pockets. He didn't turn his head to look at David, who just stood there nervously until he heard the door at the end of the hallway behind him clank shut too. David legs and arms still hurt. He took two short, hesitating steps and sat tentatively on the edge of the bench, all the way down from the end where the boy slouched.

David looked cautiously over at the boy. He didn't look any older than sixteen, David thought, not much older than some of my students. Same age as Jesus. The boy kept staring down at the tips of his worn, high topped sneaks and David quickly turned his own eyes back away from him. Don't want to piss him off, even if they took away all of his valuables, which were probably knives and crack pipes.

David took one quick glance back to make sure the boy didn't have any shoelaces either.

The skinny man lying on the smooth cement floor had a blue nylon windbreaker stretched up and pulled all the way around his head and he had tucked his knees up into his chest. He was snoring loudly now and David began to smell the foul odor of cheap alcohol filling the room from his open mouth.

The boy pushed himself up off the bench, took a long step forward and kicked his foot up against the sleeping man's back, then jostled him back and forth a couple times with his heel until the man stopped snoring. The boy looked at David as he turned back to sit on the bench, but his face was expressionless beyond what looked to David like a permanent resentment at the world. I hope I don't do anything to piss this kid off, David thought.

David sat on the edge of his metal seat for the next two hours and hardly moved. His mind kept grasping at all the little details of the morning – Fontagne's yelling, Schneider's surprise arrival, Donnelly putting the cuffs on him, the peacock tattoo – but he could not make sense of any of the confusion of the last four hours.

Nothing seemed to fit in place. There was no answer he could find, no explanation for anything that had just happened to him. Not one reassuring, comforting, sturdy fact.

No matter how many times he ran through every little detail, he really had no idea what to think. The idea that everyone -- Schneider, Harrison, Menendez, Borman, Fontagne, even the weasel bureaucrats downtown at the Board of Ed. offices – were all in this together against him seemed too unbelievable, but he couldn't find anything that suggested otherwise. What was he going to do?

He was going to sue them all. That's what he was going to do.

And he was going to continue teaching. Maybe not so many of the kids from this terrible neighborhood would then end up like the boy down there at the other end of the bench from him. Jesus.

He heard the door at the end of the hallway open, and the officer from the desk came down the walkway and yelled "Weintraub" before he opened the cell door. The boy never looked up. The man on the floor kept breathing heavily, his face against the concrete wall.

"Time to go downtown," the officer said and he put his hand around David's arm to guide him back toward the door he'd just come in through.

"Downtown?" David asked.

"Central Booking," the cop said. "Ya know, downtown."

David thought, The Tombs? He'd heard about that place. Every gangbanger, crack dealer, junkie, knife slashing teen he'd heard about from his students who'd gotten busted around the neighborhood got processed in at the Tombs. Or Riker's Island.

Oh, please, no, not Riker's Island, David thought, as the officer put the handcuffs back on him and led him out to the large white van that had backed up to the rear door of the precinct. He knew about Riker's Island, reputed to be the largest penal colony in the country, one that housed real criminals. Real criminals, oh my God, David thought.

He climbed into the shiny metal chamber that was the back of the van and sat on the bench seat right behind where the driver would be. A young officer with perfectly trimmed black sideburns and a shotgun with a polished wood stock sat down across from him. A second later Freddie Donnelly climbed up the rear steps into the windowless chamber and sat down next to David.

"Hi, Mr. Weintraub," he said happily. "I'm going to go with you and get you processed downtown, seeing as you're my arrest."

"At least you're a familiar face, Freddie," David said.

Donnelly leaned in close to him.

"Probably best if you don't call me 'Freddie' in front of these people," he said.

"Right. Of course. How was it you were the one to arrest me?"

"Well, Mr. W, I've got the authority. We decided to arrest you back at the school and the precinct guys asked me if I wanted to make the arrest."

"I didn't know you could make an arrest, you know, just being a safety and security officer."

Donnelly bristled.

"Mr. Weintraub, I'm deputized, you know."

"How was it you decided to arrest me before you even asked me my version of what happened?"

"We already had probable cause."

"Probable cause? What probable cause?"

"Fontagne's complaint."

"Did you see any wound on her?"

"No, not really."

"Did you see a weapon?"

"No, Mr. Weintraub. We had her statement."

"What if she was lying?" David asked.

Freddie thought about that for a moment.

"I don't think she was. Neither did Harrison or Schneider. This is my first arrest, you know. These precinct guys let me do it."

David wondered if the police from the precinct had wanted nothing to do with Fontagne's complaint or David's arrest, having already gone through the phony sexual assault charge with David by the school authorities earlier that spring. Detective Sweeney had known the school was out to get David. Maybe those two cops knew it too.

None of the police and court personnel he was about to face knew anything about that, though. They were going to think he was a real criminal. And treat him like one.

One, two, three, four, five, six, seven.

Twenty minutes later the van bumped once, bouncing David on the seat, and then it stopped and started backing up. When it stopped again, the back door opened and David saw a uniformed policeman holding open the door of the building just a few feet from the van's door. David could see the long corridor behind him.

After he stepped down from the van, David glanced around behind him and saw a tall chain link fence, at least fifteen feet high, topped with concertina wire, surrounding the parking area they had pulled into.

"No sightseeing," the cop at the door said, and David felt Donnelly start pushing against his back to get him into the building, the skin on his wrists tender again from the abrasive handcuffs.

The policeman led David and Donnelly into a small elevator and in its cramped space the three of them descended one or two floors, David couldn't tell which, and arrived facing an open bay after the elevator door snapped open.

"It's okay. We've got him now," the NY policemen said to Donnelly. "Thanks, Officer…" he looked down at the plastic nametag pinned to Freddie's chest, "…Donnelly."

Donnelly removed David's handcuffs, attached them back to his own leather belt and started back over to the elevator. After he'd pushed the up button, he turned back to David.

"Don't worry, Mr. Weintraub. Everything'll be alright," he said.

David wasn't so sure.

CHAPTER 8

"Weintraub?"

An officer with a clipboard in his hand called out to David.

"Yes, sir."

"Come with me. I need fingerprints, a mug shot and your medical information."

"I already had my fingerprints taken back at the precinct station," David offered.

"They lose everything up there. We take our own here. Go stand up against the wall, feet on that X painted on the floor."

David walked nervously over to the concrete block wall, turned and backed up until he felt the solidity of the cool surface against his shoulders. A bright light suddenly flashed in his face and the office called out, "You're done. Over here." He pointed to the fingerprint counter on his left.

"Am I going to get to eat soon?" David asked as he held out his right index finger.

"Does this look like a Denny's to you?" the officer barked. "You're gonna get processed in right now, go to the holding cell, be called up before the judge – hopefully by the end of the night – and either given bail, released or sent on to Riker's if you can't make bail. If you're lucky, you'll get some breakfast there tomorrow morning." The officer eyed the bulge of David's midsection. "But it probably won't be enough for a big guy like you."

"I'm hungry," David said. "Isn't there a vending machine here?"

"You a diabetic?"

"No, sir."

"Then you're shit out of luck, son."

The officer finished taking David's fingerprints, gave him a rag and led him over to a desk on the other side of the crowded room. As the man got the paperwork ready for David to fill out, David watched as other prisoners were brought down by the elevator, ready to be processed in. One officer would break away from of the group of policemen standing at the far side of the room, talking and joking, and check in each new arrival.

"When do I get my phone call?" David asked.

"You want to make a phone call?" the officer asked, as if that were an even stranger request than wanting to eat.

"Yes, I do. That's not just something you see on TV, is it?"

"You some kind of smartass?" the officer said, his eyes still focused on the forms down on the desk in front of him as he got them ready for David.

"Smart, yes. Smartass, no," David said.

The policeman looked up at David and stared at his face for a second.

"Okay, then. We can do that right now." He handed David the receiver from the phone on his desk. "What's the number?"

David gave him his father's number and sat there without moving, listening to it ring. He hoped he wouldn't choke up when his father answered. Instead, he heard his father's voice mail message. David swore once and then began speaking.

"Dad, I've been arrested. First at the local precinct, now I'm at the main Brooklyn Processing center. Can you get me out of here? Quickly. I don't want to spend the night in jail. I really don't want to go to Riker's Island." He began choking up a bit. He couldn't think of anything else to say and then he heard the answering machine shut off.

"My father's a lawyer," David told the officer.

"I see. Okay, let's get to this paperwork."

When they were done, the officer called out "This one's ready" to another policeman who was standing by a thick metal sliding door at the back of the room. He came over and the officer David grabbed him by the top of one shoulder to pull his ear close to him and spoke, but David couldn't make out what he said.

"Come with me then," the second officer said and led David through the metal door and down a dark corridor with light bulbs in little metal cages every few feet along the ceiling.

As they walked, David began to notice the smell of human body odor, warm garbage and some other distasteful scents he couldn't identify. They turned a corner at the end of the long damp hallway and David faced a wall of grey steel bars at the other end of a large room with two desks, each with a policeman sitting at it.

Behind the floor to ceiling bars were about forty men, some sitting with their backs to the far wall, some lying on the floor sleeping, others standing around in groups of four or five, talking. David realized he would be the only white man in there. Token honky prisoner, he thought to himself, and remembered Lisa's comments about herself in Bushwick.

He wished he could talk to her now. He was scared.

The officer led him over to the cell door, unlocked it and guided David in. David heard the lock clink shut behind him, but he didn't move. He looked for a vacant spot along one of the back walls of the large cell and saw a place between two groups of black men where he thought he could stand safely. He walked, almost on his tiptoes, arms stiff by his sides, across the floor, skirting around five Latino boys standing together in the middle of the cell, and spun around quickly when he reached the wall. He pushed his back up against it.

One or two prisoners had looked up at him when he first entered the cell, but no one was paying any attention to him after he'd huddled against the wall.

I wish I wasn't so big, David thought. I don't want to stand out at all, but then he realized no one else in the cell cared. To these guys, he was invisible. None of them had ever read his davefromqueens blog, he was sure.

There were several clusters of young black men with dreadlocks or do-rags standing, talking together in twos and threes around the cell. Several more sat propped up against the back wall or had curled up on the floor to sleep. The Latino gangbangers stood together in larger groups – maybe based on their gang affiliation, David thought – and moved their bodies and arms in quick, awkward staccato movements as they talked to each other.

At one point a young man with "Amor de Rey" tattooed across the left side of his neck was brought in and he was greeted by a rapid flurry of finger signs from one of the two large Latino groups massed together on the other side of the cell.

Who knows what these people are in here for, David thought. Drugs, robbery, assault – assault by something more serious than a pencil – maybe even murder. Some of these kids were so young, though, barely older than his students, but now victims of the same New York school system that had removed him from the classroom, removed these boys' only hope for not becoming a gangbanger or ending up here in jail. He thought of Jesus and wondered if he had passed through this same cell that day he'd stabbed Elias in the eye.

Now I'm the one who's here, not Jesus, David realized, and he resolved again to get back into a classroom as soon as he could.

As well as sue those bastards.

David kept moving his eyes back and forth between groups so he could be prepared if some fight broke out or if one of these young street boys decided to taunt him, just because they felt like it. He had been used to that as a kid in school in Port Jefferson, of course, being called "Jew Boy" or "Bagel Boy." He could handle that. But what if one of these guys wanted to rough him up a bit?

Sure, he was bigger than anybody in the cell, but he couldn't defend himself against one of these street kids. They'd cream him, and if the others all stood around him to hide what was going on, the guards sitting out there at their desks would never notice until it was too late.

He consoled himself with the thought that if he had made it through six months of sensory deprivation torture at the district office, he could make it through at least the next six or so hours here. As long as nothing terrible happened.

He'd just have to remain invisible. Invisible, right, he thought. In his blue oxford cloth button down shirt and tan Dockers. He looked around the cell. Yup, he was the only guy in there not wearing black. Maybe that's why he was invisible to them. He didn't even have a tattoo.

He pushed his back up against the wall and breathed deeply until the stench of the cell made him gag. He noticed a polished aluminum toilet over in the far corner of the cell. It had become stuffed to overflowing with fruit peelings and wadded toilet paper, and for several feet around it the smooth concrete floor was covered in urine, dirt and other dark liquids. David didn't want to guess what they were.

He pursed his lips together and tried to keep breathing deeply enough to be calmed, but not so deeply that the air's foul smells would make him gag again.

David stood with his back against the wall for hours. He'd lift one foot up and place his sole against the wall behind him for awhile, and then do the same with the other to relieve the pain and stiffness that set in to the thick muscles of his back. He was hungry and he was tired, but his fear kept him alert for a long time, until a haze began to settle over his mind and he felt his eyelids flutter and close before they suddenly sprung open again and he'd feel terror again for a second.

He no longer was sure how long he'd been there.

New prisoners would be brought into the cell and sometimes a guard would come to the door and yell out a name and a boy would break away from one of the groups and be escorted out. At one point David thought he saw his father talking to one of the policemen at the desk on the other side of the cell door, but David couldn't tell if he'd just nodded out and dreamed it or if his father had actually been there.

It was a long night, and he didn't know how much longer he could go on standing, but he still didn't dare just sit down on the floor with his back against the wall. He'd be too easy a target. At least standing, the guards could still see him head and shoulders above the others there.

He forced his eyes to open wider and he began scanning back and forth across the cell, as he would do driving by himself late at night, just willing himself to stay awake and alert. One, two, three, four, five, six, seven.

As the hours passed, David imagined himself as Gandhi, on one of his fourteen day fasts, protesting the oppressive British government, and at moments David began to feel a shimmery, almost out of body experience as he stood with his back pressed lightly against the cool concrete wall. He was becoming more and more lightheaded.

Startled, David had no idea what time it was when he heard the guard call out "Weintraub" from the cell door. He made his way slowly and stiffly around the sleeping bodies and let the guard fasten the handcuffs, his hands in front of him this time, before he was led upstairs on the elevator to one of the courtrooms on the fifth floor. The guard remained with him and the two of them stood in a line of other guards escorting prisoners to wait their turn in front of the judge. The black Roman numerals on the white clock face above them read 11:40.

David felt alert again with a new rush of fear from not knowing what the judge would say to him, what questions he'd be asked, what answers he'd have to come up with so he wouldn't have to spend the rest of the night in jail, let alone be carted off to Riker's Island.

He read the name plate on the polished wood counter in front of the judge. Morris Rabinowitz, Judge, Fifth District Court. Score one for our side, at least, David thought to himself, and then he noticed his father standing with a group of other lawyers, David presumed, on the opposite side of the court room waiting their turns in front of the judge.

In front of them a thin woman in a black pants suit and white blouse with dark stringy hair stood by a long table stacked high with folders. The DA, David figured. She looked exhausted.

After the three prisoners in front of him had gone before the judge, one by one, and had been escorted back out through the courtroom doors – none of them had anyone there to make bail for them and they were all on their way to Riker's – David stepped up in front of the judge, handcuffs on, guard still on his right. His father came forward, smiled slightly at David and stood on his left. They all waited while the DA and the judge finished studying David's folder and paperwork.

The judge looked up from whatever documents he had in front of him, hidden by the polished wood surface of the rail at David's eye level, and looked at David for several seconds.

He's certainly judging, David thought.

"Ms. Irwin?" the judge finally said to the DA.

"The city requests bail of three thousand dollars, your honor. It's an assault case."

"Yes, I see. Assault with a deadly…pencil?"

David heard a muffled laugh from one of the lawyers across the room.

"Yes, that's right. Might have been a broken pencil, maybe a pen. The victim says she felt a pain in her lower back."

"Were there any bruises on this…" the judge looked down and shuffled through some papers "…this Ms. Fontagne?"

"No, sir."

"Were there any marks on her skin?"

"No, sir."

"Did the victim seek any medical attention?"

"No, sir."

The judge wrote down something on the paperwork in front of him, closed the folder and then set it over to the right.

"Mr. Weintraub is to be released on is own recognizance, no bail, once he has signed an order of protection forbidding him from going near Ms. Fontagne. Next."

"Thank you, your honor," David said.

The judge nodded his head slightly and looked for a minute at David. He seemed more curious than friendly, and David felt himself breaking into tears with the relief he felt, and the tiredness, and the hunger, but he clenched his fists together and let his father guide him out of the courtroom.

On the long drive back to David's apartment in Queens, he and his father hardly spoke.

"I'll call you in a day or two," his father said as David got out of the car, "and we'll start working on our court case for real."

In his apartment David made himself a double-decker peanut butter and jelly sandwich – it was the easiest and fastest – wolfed it down and collapsed on his bed still dressed in his blue shirt and Dockers, which he realized as he fell asleep, smelled like the jail.

When his alarm went off at six the next morning, David called in to Menendez's office and used his final sick day for this last day of the school year. Then he went back to bed and pulled the covers up and over his head, still dressed. He slept all day.

"We've got ninety days to file a Notice of Claim, David," his father said as he pushed his swivel chair back from his desk and folded his hands behind his head.

"What are we claiming?" David asked. He was sitting on the orange upholstered couch by the wall that had been there since the first day he'd ever visited his father's office as a little boy. David could remember sitting happily on it, his feet dangling a foot or so above the tan shag rug while his mother had waited to get money from his dad to take him shopping for a new snowsuit and winter boots.

"Anybody who feels they've been falsely imprisoned has ninety days to file or they forfeit their right to recoup any damages," his father told him. David realized that he had never paid any attention to his father as a lawyer while growing up. Instead, he was always memorizing RBI's, passing yards or hockey goal assists. He had never known anything about what his father actually did when he left the house.

"What are we going to say are the 'damages'?" David asked.

"Oh, 'deprivation of personal liberty, counsel fees, great emotional distress, pain and suffering and fright.' Something along those lines."

"I've been having nightmares ever since that night. Should I document them somehow?"

"We'll figure that out in the actual suit we bring. Right now we just need to get this Notice of Claim done. I've been thinking, though. You should sue for having your First Amendment rights violated because of the retaliation against you after you filed those grievances."

"That's a freedom of speech issue?

"Sure. You were punished for speaking out, that is, for filing those grievances."

"Good. Let's do it. I want to nail these guys every way possible."

"We're not actually "nailing these guys" so much with a First Amendment suit. But if we win, it'll set a legal precedent that'll protect others, not to mention bringing us – I mean, my office – some bankable attention."

"Who would it protect? I should probably know these things, but you're the lawyer."

Dad's pretty smart, David thought. All those silent meals around their dinner table, with just the click of knives and forks on their plates and saucers. The only communication was Michelle and Karen signing letters to form sentences, a little something Michelle taught Karen to piss off their mother. Family gatherings had never revealed much about his father or his work.

"It'll protect the thousands, heck, maybe millions, of people who can not now voice a complaint without fear of reprisal."

"Millions? That's a lot more than the twenty-six kids in my classroom."

"Well, thank goodness, that classroom -- and the whole New York School Board of Education business -- is all behind you, now that the school year is over. You won't ever have to go through that again."

"I'm going teach again this fall, dad."

"What?" His father let his chair come forward.

"Yeah. That's what I do, dad. I teach. I'm good at it, or I would be if those bastards would put me back in the classroom. I've already started sending out resumes. I just don't want to teach under Harrington and Schneider, or Menendez, anymore."

"David, they're just going to come after you again, don't you think?"

"Not if I'm in another district. Besides, filing this other law suit should make them too scared to come after me again. I mean…"

"Maybe."

David could tell his father wanted to say more, but was withholding himself. For the first time ever, David wanted his father's advice and he waited a few seconds, but his father still didn't speak. He just relaxed back into his chair.

"Yeah, you and I both know they're pretty stupid, don't we?" David finally said.

David had been concerned that his "U" rating with the New York City school system might be a red flag for him when he applied for another teaching position, even though he was going to apply in other boroughs. He knew he didn't want to take any chances in Brooklyn itself, but not one of the schools he'd applied to even offered him an interview, and he began to feel he had a big scarlet letter "U" for Unsatisfactory tattooed across his forehead. He decided to try his previously successful tactic and go to a job fair, but this time at the very end of the summer, when schools were most desperate to fill their last open teaching positions.

He arrived in late August in the same large gymnasium he'd been to the previous summer and sat down on one of the metal folding chairs set up along one wall so he could observe everything that was going on before he worked out his strategy for the morning.

Each district appeared to have its own area on the gymnasium floor with individual tables set up for each of the schools in that district. One or two staff sat at each table and either waited for someone to show up or interviewed someone when they did, but there weren't nearly the number of applicants as the previous summer, David noticed. He didn't know if that would increase or decrease his chances – because now he would stand out more – but he was more concerned that his reputation from 232 had somehow preceded him here.

As he watched the staff from the different districts talk with each other and with the applicants who were being interviewed at each district's tables, one group of two older men in shirtsleeves and a young woman in designer jeans looked to David like they were actually having fun together. If there was no applicant in front of them, they'd be laughing or joking or punching each other playfully in the shoulders. The handwritten sign on their table read P.S. 67, The Bronx. Some Bronx neighborhoods were even rougher than Bushwick, David had heard.

He watched them carrying on with each other and then one young, obviously nervous woman sat down at their table to be interviewed. Within a couple minutes she, too, was smiling and laughing, and David decided that was the table he was going to.

When the young woman left, he made a bee line across the polished wood floor and offered his resume to one of the two older men.

"Well, sit down, David," the man said after looking down at the resume. "You're a real veteran, I bet, eh? Down in the trenches there in Bushwick. Don't see any obvious battle scars on you though. You survived, huh?"

"I'm still alive and kicking," David said. "What positions do you have open? The Bronx would be a commute for me, from Bayside, but what they hey. I just got a little Ford Escort. Used, but nice."

Ten minutes later David was on his way over to a table by the front doors with a computer set up on it to have his information entered and his name marked as a new teacher at P.S. 67, just off Jerome Avenue, one of the worst neighborhoods in the south Bronx.

Please, don't let there be some alarm that goes off when they enter my name into the New York Schools database, David thought. Please, please.

He sat down at the table and handed his paperwork to the woman at the keyboard.

"Congratulations, Mr. Weintraub, on your new position. This will just take a couple of minutes while I enter all this in as a new hire for 67."

David held his breath as he watched her type his name, address, phone and social security number from the form she had set down next to her on the table.

Nothing. No buzzing. No big flashing "Rejected" on the screen. No "U." Nothing.

He was in.

Three days later he received a letter from the Chancellor of the New York City Board of Education welcoming him and inviting him to attend the New York School system conference for new teachers at the Hilton Hotel on West 51st the following Monday. He knew he would never have received that letter or been invited to that conference if someone in Menendez' district had contaminated his file in the main computer with data about his Unsatisfactory rating or about his two arrests.

Good, the cancer has been contained to Bushwick, he thought, and he fished the little tin cannon out of his Dockers pocket and placed it back inside the worn Monopoly box on his shelf.

"This is a pretty bad neighborhood," the Assistant Principal, Doug

Fisher, said to David as he toured him around the hallways of P.S. 67, "but we all band together here to give these kids the best chance they'll ever have. Sometimes we win, sometimes we fail."

"I know those odds pretty well," David said.

Fisher was a thin, red-haired man whose fair skin made David think he was not much older than David himself, but he was so relaxed, it was hard to believe he carried all the responsibilities of an assistant principal. David was impressed.

As Fisher poked his head in one classroom after another, teachers paused and gave him a big smile or wave, and some of the kids called out "Good morning, Mr. Fisher" to him. In the cafeteria he joked with the two older black women who were preparing lunch about what was on the menu for the day and if he was going to have to eat steamed spinach again. One of them told him he needed as much spinach as he could get to put some color back into that pale face of his.

Fisher introduced David to them and to everyone else he ran into in the halls and the offices. By the end of the morning David felt like he'd arrived home.

He was assigned to be a Cluster Teacher, one of a group of sixteen teachers in the school who filled in for the regular teachers when they were on their preparation time. Fisher warned him that a Cluster Teacher was more likely to have control problems in the classroom because he or she wasn't the regular teacher, but the good news was there was virtually no preparation time for Cluster Teachers and when they went home for the day. They had no "homework" themselves.

With no evening class preparation, David started spending more time grooming his political blogs and doing research at the Touro law library, which had also come to feel like a home to him. Sometimes after school he'd shoot over to New Jersey or up to Connecticut to play a little poker at one of the casinos he liked, even though with their bright lights and neon glitter they never felt like any kind of home to him.

By the end of his second week teaching, to his surprise, he began to be complimented by other teachers and staff. Doug Fisher made a point of seeking him out in the break room one morning to tell him he was doing a great job and that the principal herself had heard how well he was interacting with the kids.

"Keep up that good work, David," he said and when David said, "Thank you, sir," Fisher responded with "Cut that out, David. Just call me Doug, will ya?"

Other Cluster Teachers and regular teachers also let him know that they "had heard good things" about him. Teaching was becoming the dream David had always wanted it to be.

The kids loved him, too, and David started spending time in the evenings, even though he didn't have to, preparing new little classroom "events" to keep his kids looking at and learning about the world around them.

At the end of September one of the new regular teachers gave her notice. She had been assigned a class full of students with discipline problems and low performance histories and despite all the support she received from her peers, it was too much for her.

That afternoon Fisher called David into his office, shook his hand and told him he was going to be her replacement.

David called his sister Michelle as soon as he got home that night and told her he finally found a school where he felt like he was at home. He was happy. And, by the way, did she have any new good-looking girlfriends she could introduce him to?

On Friday afternoon of the first week in October, Doug Fisher came up to David as he left the teacher's lounge, ready to go back to his classroom after lunch. Nobody in that neighborhood had sautéed peppers on their grinders, but he had found a nearby deli that had great pastrami sandwiches. And great Cherry Cola, too.

"David," Doug said, "The Deputy Superintendent in the Chancellor's Office, Frank Santini, wants to see you downtown immediately. Room 301 there. Something about your fingerprints and having been arrested. Anything I should do for you?" He looked surprised, but concerned.

"A long story, Doug. And obviously, getting longer. I'll tell you about it later."

As David drove across the Triborough Bridge from Brooklyn into Manhattan to make his way down to the New York City Board of Education offices, he knew there was something fishy about this. When his name had been entered into the computer at the job fair that August, nothing had been triggered, and nothing on file at the Chancellor's office had prevented them from sending him a welcome letter. Now this. What was up?

He found a parking lot about three blocks from the offices, walked back to the Board of Ed. building and took the elevator up to the third floor. Nervous, he walked down the hallway to his left until he realized the office numbers were going up, turned and went back past the elevator. He found Room 301 and entered.

"I'm David Weintraub," he said to the young secretary. "Mr. Santini asked me to come down to meet him."

"Just a second," the woman said and whispered something into the intercom on her desk.

A thin man in his fifties with a full head of thick black hair, perfectly

111

cut, came out of the back office and offered David his hand.

"Frank Santini," he said.

David was surprised at Santini's limp handshake and knew things were not going to be good when the man looked away from David's eyes as he told him he'd have to wait for just a minute.

This guy's really creepy, David thought.

"You can wait out in the hallway, Mr. Weintraub," the secretary said after Santini had disappeared back into his office. "There's a bench just across the hall."

David went out into the hall and paced back and forth for several minutes, wondering who Santini had to call to prepare himself for this meeting. Menendez? Harrison? Both? After a few minutes of pacing David finally went and sat on the wooden bench that seemed much too small for him. He tapped his feet, he patted his thighs, he clenched his fists and tried to hold back the anger that he felt building up in him.

I am not happy about this, he kept repeating to himself. I am not happy about this.

Another half an hour passed before the secretary popped her head out the door and told him, "The Deputy Superintendent is ready to see you now." She held the door open as David rushed into the front office and went right back through Santini's doorway.

Santini remained seated behind his desk and didn't offer David a seat in either of the two red leather chairs facing him.

"Mr. Weintraub, I'm going to have to terminate you because of your criminal record and because your fingerprints are bad." He spoke quietly, as if a calm voice might subdue David, who stood in front of him, face flushed, arms trembling with his contained anger.

"I have no criminal record," David said. "I have a misdemeanor charge pending against me. The charge is false and will be dismissed on the merits." David loved being able to use the new legal phrase he had recently learned from his father.

"But did you inform your school, you know, P.S. 67, about your arrest?"

"I gave them all the information necessary. If you check your computer, you'll see I have no criminal record and my fingerprints are not bad. What do you mean, anyway, by 'my fingerprints are bad'?"

"Look," Santini said, "This didn't come from my office. I'm just doing what I was, uh, told and telling you that you can't come back until this fingerprint situation is cleared up."

"What 'fingerprint situation'? You mean, that I do not have a criminal record, but that I've been arrested?"

"I don't know what to tell you. I'm just doing what, uh, Mr. Stefanik at the office of Personnel Investigations told me. He's the Chief

Administrator over there."

"But my fingerprints were just cleared when I was hired at 67."

"Yes, but then if you got arrested subsequently..."

"But I'd been arrested prior to when I was hired."

"That I don't know. I mean, I'm not doubting what you are saying. I'm not doubting it might be accurate. I have no knowledge of that. I mean I just know you're telling me that."

"What I'm telling you is that, yes, I've been arrested, but no, I have no criminal record. Frankly, I thought that in this country there was still a presumption of innocence."

"I don't know what to tell you. At the moment you're terminated. My job is to protect the children. You can appreciate that?"

"Protect the children? What disturbs me the most about all this, Deputy Superintendent, is that right now, today, there are twenty-six children who are not getting the education they're entitled to."

"You mean the twenty-six children who will not now have you as their teacher?"

"Exactly."

"Mr. Weintraub, I can't put you in the classroom until your fingerprints are cleared. That's the law. I can't help that. I can't change that. This is all out of my hands."

"But why wouldn't my fingerprints be cleared if I don't have a criminal record?"

"That's assuming you were arrested. Assuming you were arrested. I don't know if that's the case." Santini had been sitting without moving behind his desk, his hands hidden on his lap from David, but now his voice became increasingly agitated and David noticed moisture on his clean shaven upper lip. "If you were arrested, it came up as a possible felony conviction."

"There is no pending felony charge."

David felt his shoulders relax and his anger subside with the sudden certainty that he was absolutely right here, and he could tell Santini knew it too.

"I don't know," Santini said, his fingers now playing with a pen that lay on the blotter on his desk. "Like I said, this is all, uh, out of my hands. You're going to have to see Mr. Stefanik to get cleared to go back in the classroom."

"And where is he?"

"Downstairs on the first floor, all the way at the end of the hallway, on the right."

"Thank you."

Santini is such a puppet, David thought, as he waited in the hallway for the elevator to bring him down to the first floor. Guess I'm about to

Michelle Riklan and Karen Weintraub

find out if Stefanik is the one pulling his strings. This ought to be good.

114

CHAPTER 9

This guy's even creepier than Santini, David thought, as soon as he saw the head of Personnel Investigations appear in the doorway of his office and beckon him in. The man looked like the floor boss of the afternoon shift at Bally's. Tight, shiny black suit, crisp white shirt, thin black tie and Dean Martin hair. He was smiling, but David already knew not to trust that friendly expression. The man's eyes told a different story.

"Mr. Santini just phoned me. You need some further explanation for your termination?" Stefanik said. He'd stopped just inside his office door to face David.

"It seems the facts you have about my pending charges are incorrect," David said.

"Incorrect? I don't think so. I just checked. Our office had sent a letter to Menendez last July recommending your 'reassignment' until your Assault in the Second Degree case was resolved."

"But I was never arraigned on Assault in the Second Degree."

"Are you doubting my word," Stefanik asked, the smile still on his face. "I heard you'd applied to P.S. 67 for a position right after Menendez got that letter. What did you think? You could just go somewhere else and get your tenure?"

"I went to the Chancellor's Office job fair and my application was run through your computer, just like everybody else." David had started scraping his feet back and forth on the thick carpet in Stefanik's front office, like a bull getting ready to charge, but he knew he'd better control his rage at the bureaucrat in front of him, sleazy as he was.

"Weintraub, you're unemployable here, pure and simple."

David stood there, looking Stefanik in the face, and waited for a few seconds before he spoke so he could let the rush of angered thoughts in his mind settle down.

"Perhaps it's best if you speak to my father about this. He's also my lawyer.'

"Sure. Have him call me. Now, I think we're done here."

"Yes, we are." David said and turned to walk out of Stefanik's office.

"Have a good day, Mr. Weintraub," he heard as he rushed past the secretary's desk.

"I talked to Stefanik," David's dad told him on the phone two days later. He was standing at the window of his Long Island office watching the November snow falling gently on the hood of his Lexus in the little parking area next to his office.

"And?"

"You're still terminated, I'm afraid."

"So what's next?"

"I called Billy O'Brien -- he's a union official I've represented a couple times – to ask him who this Stefanik is. I guess he's been the hatchet man for the Board of Ed. for almost thirty years. Billy said he's screwed over hundreds of people, in and out of the school system. No conscience. No humanity. A prick, if you will."

"So what's next?"

"We're going to court. They've exposed their throat to us now. You know, legally, they could have just fired you without giving a reason -- said simply you weren't the kind of teacher they were looking for -- but now they've committed themselves on paper to firing you because of the court charges. Large error on their part. Add to that our case for their retaliation against you for your filing that first grievance and we've got a solid, solid case."

"There's a new tactic they're using against me too. I forgot to tell you. They owed me pay for the end of August to the first of October for PS 67. They deposited nine hundred of it, but then they withdrew that money from my account. And now they're giving me the run around on paying me anything more that they owe me."

"How are you living then? I mean, financially."

"I thought I was going to get unemployment, but over there they said I'm not qualified because I was discharged because of misconduct...you know, my arrest record. I'd figured I'd collect for a couple months until the charges are thrown out and I can return to teaching, but now they're denying me that income. I'm doing okay in Atlantic City, though."

"What's the name of the person you're dealing with at the Department of Labor?"

"Mrs. O'Hara. At the Livingstone Street office."

"I'll write her an official letter tomorrow, challenging her adjudication."

"Do you think that all these city departments are coordinating their attack on me?"

"I honestly don't know. I hope not. It could just be the inefficiency of an uncoordinated, and impersonal, system. But I don't know."

"You're more of an optimist than I am, Dad."

"Yeah, well, you're the one down in the trenches. I'm sitting comfortably in the Adjutant General's tent, looking down on the battle."

"I'm beginning to see that's the place to be, up there making sure everyone's playing by the rules of the game, not suffering when you find yourself with a bunch of players who cheat, bully and harass. In other words, the New York Board of Education weasels."

"So let's go after them then, get 'em to play by the rules."

David was surprised to hear his father so enthusiastic about this. That had never seemed the case to David growing up.

"So, what's next?" David asked.

"File a preliminary legal challenge to the Board of Ed. They'll have to respond to it in court, and if they respond poorly, we've got them. It's called an Article 78."

"After they respond, how long will it take to win our case?"

"I hate to tell you this, David, but it'll probably take years. I'm not going to let them settle for some quick, compromised version. I want to hold their feet to the fire for all they've done to you, but if I do, they're going to take years to drag this whole thing out. That'll be their strategy. To wear us down til we surrender."

"Do you think we'll eventually have to surrender?"

"No."

"Good. I'm ready."

David hung up the phone and looked over at the shelf of board games in his apartment. He got up and went over and got out his Monopoly cannon and slipped it into his pocket. He pushed the other tokens around in their compartment in the box with his index finger, wondering which one would best suit his dad. Automobile, iron, shoe, thimble, wheelbarrow? He had no idea. Finally, he closed the box and slid it back onto the pile on the shelf.

He'd never really known his father well enough to decide which token suited him best, and he still didn't know today. He knew, though, that without his father's help now, he would already have been chewed up into little pieces and spit out onto the streets of Bushwick by these bureaucratic weasels.

David's first court appearance was in front of Justice Foster. As part of their lawsuit against the Board of Ed. for wrongful termination, David and his father had filed a request for a temporary order reinstating David into the classroom, even though they knew their chances of having the order granted were minimal, even if their wrongful termination case was rock solid. It was not a matter of substance, it turned out, but a matter of law – what could and couldn't be ordered legally – but they chose to file the request anyway just to add one more fusillade in their attack on the Board of Ed. bureaucracy.

David and his father slid into the wooden bench in Foster's courtroom to wait for their case to be called.

"Foster's a real veteran, knows the law," David's dad leaned over and whispered to him. "He's got quite a sense of humor, too, so this should at least be entertaining, even if we don't win. That's John Bradshaw over there, lawyer for the Board of Ed. He's one of their new hire flunkies, sent over here to handle this simple court appearance."

Smith was sitting on one of the benches ahead of them and to their left. He had his briefcase open on his lap and was shuffling through and studying various papers, apparently preparing for what was to come. He turned and looked back at David once, but the light reflecting on the lens of his wire rimmed glasses hid his eyes from David's stare. David knew from Smith's crisp white button down shirt, striped tie and charcoal grey suit that, despite his young age, he was already a quintessential "company man." Weasel-in-training, David thought to himself.

"All rise," the court clerk bellowed. "The Honorable Justice Malcolm R. Foster."

A short man with a head full of unruly wisps of white hair and a neatly trimmed white beard and mustache emerged from a side door and made his way up the steps of the platform he ruled his court from.

"Alright, Henry, who's first today?" he asked the clerk.

The clerk handed up a manila folder and Foster slid his reading glasses on, opened it up and started reading. After a minute he set the folder down and looked down at David and his father and then looked over at Bradshaw. The three of them stood looking up at Foster.

"Well," he announced, "Weintraub and Weintraub here are right on the money. What's your take on this, Bradshaw?"

"Your Honor," Bradshaw began, "per New York State Law 14318…"

"Everybody in the court room knows what's in the law books, Bradshaw. What's your motion?"

"Sir, that the temporary order reinstating Mr. Weintraub to the classroom be denied. As I was going to say, New York State Law 14318…"

"Is there anybody here for the Board of Education who has at least an ounce of brains, or are we just stuck with you here today, Bradshaw?" Foster asked the young attorney, now noticeably red in the face.

"It's just me here today, Your Honor," Bradshaw said and cleared his throat several times, as if he had something disagreeable in it.

"Alright, then. Motion granted, folks. Temporary order denied. Sorry, Messieurs Weintraub, but that's the law. However, I'm pushing your wrongful termination Article 78 on to the next level." Foster took his glasses off and winked at David before turning to the other lawyer. "Now, Mr. Bradshaw, I'm going to recommend to you that someone over there at the Board of Education sit down with Mr. Weintraub and try to resolve this matter, fast, because otherwise you guys are going to have a public relations nightmare on your hands if even half the things in here are true. Someone needs to take the officials over there at the Board of Education by the scruffs of their necks and shake them until they come to an understanding as to what they ought to be doing here."

"Yes, Your Honor," Bradshaw said quietly, and when Foster waved his hand in disgust at him, he retreated to the back of the courtroom to go out through the double doors.

"Best of luck, you two," Foster said to David and his father, still standing together in front of him. "You know, you two don't really look like father and son."

"It is hard to tell," David said, "but, in fact, our livers are actually identical."

Foster hesitated a second, trying to sort out if that had been a joke or a strange non-sequitur, but he quickly laughed when he saw the smile on David's face.

"Oh, yeah," Foster said, "Now that you mention it, I can see it in the color of your eyes. Both the same brown."

"Thank you, your honor," David's father said and nudged his son with his elbow to let him know it was time to leave.

Two weeks later David was driving his father through Manhattan morning rush hour traffic for their appearance in Judge O'Reilly's courtroom, where Foster had forwarded their Article 78 case for wrongful termination.

"This morning's the money shot," David's father said to him as they inched their way through the Long Island Expressway traffic, now bunching up for the Queens-Midtown tunnel. "If our case is dismissed, it's game over, but if their motion to dismiss is denied, they're going to have to commit themselves in writing and they're going to have to be deposed. You know some of them will perjure themselves."

"This is like a big chess game, isn't it," David said, "with the New York court system our playing board?"

"I don't know, David. I never learned how to play chess."

Although they arrived half an hour before court was to convene, they found O'Reilly's courtroom already full of plaintiffs, their families and their lawyers, all waiting to see if they had presented enough evidence to move their cases on to the next level or if they were going to have them dismissed right then and there by Judge O'Reilly.

As long as there are enough facts, enough prima facie evidence, David's father had told him beforehand, the judge is obliged to further the case. Only when it's obvious there's no real evidence does the judge dismiss. I think we'll be fine, he'd told David.

David could feel the tension in the room, including his own, as he and his father squeezed into a bench in the back and sat next to an older woman, her thick overcoat collar still wrapped high up around her neck. She fidgeted with the crumpled court form she held above the large purse on her lap. The man on the other side of her was middle-aged and nondescript, but David was pretty sure he was her lawyer.

By the time Judge O'Reilly arrived in the high-ceilinged room, the morning's cold air had warmed with the shoulder to shoulder crowd filling the hard wooden benches. David was able to look over the tops of the heads of those in front of him as everyone stood. He was surprised how old and frail Judge O'Reilly looked. The man made his way slowly up the steps and the pale skin of his bald head looked smooth and white in the courtroom light. The skin on his face was wrinkled and grey.

"How old is this guy?" David whispered to his father.

"He's been around forever. Refuses to retire. Probably has nothing else to do."

"Except die."

"David, shsh!"

The clerk called up the first case and a man in his twenties, in jeans and a sweatshirt, Yankees jacket over his arm, came up with his lawyer and stood in front of the judge. O'Reilly scanned through the paperwork and asked a couple of questions with a complete lack of interest.

"Motion denied. Case dismissed," he said quietly.

The young man started to speak, his face red, but his lawyer grabbed him by the shoulder, turned him around and led him, still sputtering, out of the courtroom.

"That was strange," David's father said. "I thought there was more than enough evidence to further the case."

Several more cases came and went in front of the bench, and O'Reilly dismissed two more of them, even though David's father kept saying it seemed obvious there was plenty of reason to send them up to the next court.

"There's usually only one reason a judge would dismiss that many cases," he whispered to David. "He's lazy and he's just clearing his calendar so he has less paperwork to do preparing a case for the next level of trial. This makes me nervous."

"But we've got a good case," David whispered back.

"So did those people."

"Weintraub versus the City of New York," the clerk called out and David and his father made their way up to stand in front of Judge O'Reilly. The lawyer representing the City of New York, a handsome, silver haired man in an expensive suit, came up and stood to their left. David thought he looked impossibly confident.

"Counselor," O'Reilly said, "The city has a motion to dismiss?"

"Yes, your honor. As you can see, the Weintraub case is fraught with innuendo, opinion and allegation, but has no factual evidence to back up any of their claims of wrongful termination or retaliatory actions. The city acknowledges that the situation is, admittedly, an unfortunate one, your honor, but it does not merit a lawsuit."

"I think I'm going to have to disagree with you, counselor. This packet," he held up a manila folder thick with paperwork, "has more than enough specifics in it – not 'innuendo, opinion or'…what did you say…'allegation' -- to warrant it being continued to the next court. Motion to dismiss denied. I'm awarding Attorney Weintraub discovery and requiring the City to articulate their position in writing for the courts. Thank you, gentlemen. Next case."

David turned and gave the city lawyer a quick "take that" look, but the man's expression did not change. He nodded once at David's father, once at David, turned and walked away.

"Yes!" David said as he and his father walked out of the courtroom, loud enough for two young men at the end of their bench to give him a thumb's up as he walked by them, smiling.

"Let the depositions begin," his father said, smiling himself now, as they walked across the marble floor of the lobby, David's loud footsteps echoing through the cool air.

"Yes, and let these weasels begin to hoist themselves by their own little petards," David added, loudly enough for several people in the lobby to stop and watch him as he strolled across the marble floor, cordovans slapping loudly, and out through the massive front doors.

Early the next Monday morning they were driving back into Manhattan for their third court appearance.

"If today goes well," David's father said, "and I have no reason to believe it won't, we will be home free. I'll begin arranging for the depositions tomorrow."

"Yup, today's the last of the trifecta," David said.

"Trifecta? You don't gamble on horses, too, David, do you?"

"Nope. Just poker. It's the only sure thing."

"Sure thing for you, maybe. You count cards?"

"Dad, I'm not sayin'."

David's assault case was the first on the docket that morning and the clerk motioned for them to come up to the bench as soon as Judge Kaszynski was announced and seated. An athletic looking young lawyer with light brown hair still bleached from the previous summer's sun -- or Thanksgiving in Cancun, David thought -- walked up to the bench and announced himself as Martin Nelson, the representing attorney from the DA's office.

"Mr. Nelson," Kaszynski said, "the DA's Office has not submitted any paperwork in response to Mr. Weintraub's innocent plea to these charges. Why not?"

David knew that they probably hadn't submitted any because they really had no case here and he began to feel some sympathy for Nelson as he stumbled through his answer.

"Your Honor, the District Attorney is aware of the, uh, unusual nature of this particular case" -- he looked over at David as if he himself was the "unusual nature"—"and we have decided, rather than, uh, respond with the conventional documentation to instead offer Mr. Weintraub an Adjournment of Contemplative Dismissal."

"Mr. Weintraub, are you familiar with that legal device?" Kaszynski asked David.

"My father, my lawyer here, probably is, but perhaps you should explain it to me."

"If you accept the District Attorney's offer to resolve these charges in this manner, you forfeit your right to sue them and in exchange they will take no criminal action against you, provided you stay out of any further trouble for six months. At that point the case is dismissed forever without any adjudication of guilt. Understood?"

"Yes, Your Honor, I understand, but I don't accept the offer because I am, in fact, innocent. And I just might want to sue them."

"Alright, Mr. Weintraub," Kaszynski said and turned to Nelson. "Counselor?"

"Your Honor, in that case we request a week's extension in order to be able to adequately be able to prepare our case."

"You mean, to make the preparation you did not adequately make before showing up here today? Preparation for this extremely complex, 'half a pencil' case?"

Nelson went red.

"Yes, sir."

"You've got one week then," Kaszynski said. "See you all next Monday morning. Next case."

The following Monday morning Nelson, David and his father were standing in front of Kaszynski again.

"Mr. Nelson, you may begin," Kaszynski said.

"Your Honor, I'd like to request, if you don't mind, an extension until this afternoon. The District Attorney has not had time to prepare the papers for this morning, but should have them by later this afternoon."

Kaszynski looked at the young attorney, red faced again, in disbelief.

"I already gave your office a one week extension. Do they know what 'one week' means, Nelson?"

"Yes. Seven days, I believe, sir."

"Exactly. One week means one week. Seven days, no more, no less. You have no response. Weintraub's motion is granted. This case is dismissed. You're a free man, Mr. Weintraub. I thank you for showing up again this morning and I apologize for the inconvenience to you. Good day, gentlemen. Next."

David's father could hear him repeating "Yes, yes, yes, yes!" as they walked down the aisle between the benches to the courtroom doors, but he did nothing to quiet his son down.

From Manhattan they drove back out to the hospital in Queens so they could meet David's new nephew, Josh, who had been born the day before to his sister Michelle.

"I feel bad we didn't go out there last night," David said as they endured the afternoon's stop-and-go traffic on the Long Island Expressway.

"David, we had to prepare for court today."

"I know, but I still feel bad."

"Do you know how wiped out your sister probably was last night?"

"No. How wiped out?"

"She delivered a baby, for heaven's sakes."

"I thought it was just hard on the baby -- you know, like with me, not breathing and all -- not on the mother."

"It's not an area of life there are a lot of rules about."

"Guess not. All the rules come in after. Sit up at the table. Respect your elders. No running in the hallway. It's okay to walk all over the little guy."

"Well, hopefully Michelle's doing well this afternoon," David's father said.

The next morning David knew he might be on the phone for a while. He placed his yellow pad and two Bic pens on the coffee table in front of him, made sure there was a working battery in the tape recorder next to him and settled down into his sofa. He picked up the phone, ready to dial his first call.

He didn't think he was supposed to be recording calls, at least not without telling the person on the other end they were being recorded, but he figured he could at least use the tape recording to make notes from, rather than trusting his own memory, and claim in court his notes came from what he'd remembered of the call.

It was a lie, yes, but the other side was lying too.

They'd been corrupted by the system – and some of them had been corrupting the system – and now he was being corrupted too, he realized. He knew it wasn't right, but could he fight back against them all and still, himself, play by the rules? That, he didn't know, but he decided he couldn't go the other way any more.

He'd recorded other calls before, he'd snuck into Schneider's office and copied Schneider's personal notes, but now that everything was going to be put down in official documents and submitted to the New York judicial system, he decided he'd better be completely above board.

He and Lisa had been wrong.

He stood, reached down and picked up his tape recorder and took it into his bedroom and put it in the bottom drawer of his desk. Ghandi would have done the same, he thought, and he went back to the sofa, sat down and dialed Stefanik. The secretary put him through immediately.

"Mr. Stefanik," David said, "I wanted to see if you'd received the Certificate of Disposition from the court dismissing the charges against me."

David had now waited two weeks after appearing in Kaszynski's court to make sure the notification would have gone out before he called.

"Yes, Mr. Weintraub, we received that paperwork last week, in fact."

"And so that means I can be returned to the classroom?" David asked.

"Of course. I've already informed the Corporation Counsel at the Board of Ed."

But you weren't going to tell me that, were you, David thought, unless I asked you point blank, you weasel.

"So, what do I, myself, have to do to begin teaching again?"

"Nothing. Our office just needs to know that P.S. 67 still wants you and that there is a position open for you."

"And how would they know to tell you that?"

"They wouldn't, I guess, would they?"

"I'll call the Vice Principal Fisher there to let him know he needs to provide your office with that information."

"You're allowed to do that, yes," Stefanik said.

David hung up and called Doug Fisher, after calling his father to make sure there was no legal jeopardy in his contacting Fisher directly. David was playing by the rules, all the rules, now.

"Hi, Doug," David said after Fisher had come to the phone. "I don't know if you'd heard, but all the charges against me were thrown out. I can return to work there now, but the Chancellor's Investigation unit needs to know that, one, you want me, and two, that there's a position open for me."

"Yes on both accounts," Doug said. "Glad to hear they threw that thing out of the courts."

"Can you contact Stefanik's office, then, and let them know those two things?"

"I'll call them as soon as we hang up, but you need to know I can't put you back on the payroll until you've been cleared by Santini's office. He can call me and tell me verbally now that you're cleared -- just so we can get the paperwork rolling here -- but we'll also need something in writing because Santini sent us a letter in October saying you were no longer eligible to teach. We need to clear that up in writing. You know, paperwork, files up to date, written records, all that kind of bureaucratic stuff we've got to do."

"Alright. I'll call Santini while you call Stefanik."

"Will do. It'll be great to have you back here, David. Everybody loves you."

David hung up and called Santini's office. After staying on hold for nearly five minutes, David heard Santini's nervous voice answer.

"Yes? Mr. Weintraub?"

"Sir, I need you to call Vice Principal Fisher at P.S. 67 to let him know I've been cleared again to teach since the charges against me have been dropped. You knew that, right?"

"We received notification from the court, yes. I can call him, but I need to know first if they want you back and if there's a position open for you."

David wondered if Santini had been on the phone with Stefanik while David had been on hold just now.

"I just got off the phone with Fisher," David said, "and it's 'yes' to both those points. Can you just call him to give verbal approval until you get him the written reinstatement?"

"Sure. I can call him."

"Today?"

"Alright. I'll call him today."

David hung up, picked the yellow pad up off the coffee table in front of him and began writing down everything that had just happened. Later that afternoon he called Doug Fisher back to make sure Santini had called him.

"Yeah," Doug said. "He called not long after you and I had hung up. You must have some kind of clout over him now, huh? We just have to wait for his letter of reinstatement. I'll call you as soon as we get it."

"Thanks, Doug."

David was feeling pretty smug. Everything was going his way. And he was playing by the rules. He loved it.

In the mornings that followed David and his father worked on putting together the questions they'd want answered in the videotaped depositions that would be done for their court case. In the afternoons David was spending as much time as he could with his new nephew Josh.

The holiday season soon took over the rest of David's time and it was the first of the year before he realized he hadn't heard back from Doug Fisher before their Christmas break. He called Doug the first January morning after school had resumed.

"David, I was actually about to call you," Doug said when he answered his phone. "The principal here got a call yesterday from Stefanik's secretary at Personnel Investigations. She said that you won't be released to work because you have a lawsuit pending against the Board of Education. Good for you, by the way, but she said you'll need to be cleared by 'legal,' whoever they might be."

"These guys are such weasels. None of this is legal. None of this is right."

"Well, I'm glad you're taking them on. I know it's a David against Goliath situation – pardon the pun – but if you take them to task for this harassment, it might go a little easier on the rest of us in the future. Thank you for doing what you're doing."

"I'd say it was my pleasure, but it really isn't. Let me know if you hear anything more from Stefanik's office, will ya?"

"You got it. Good luck."

David hung up and immediately called his dad to fill him in on the latest oppression.

"You know what? I've had it," his father told him and hung up.

David continued to work with his father in a back room of his offices on the questions for the depositions. He would write out the questions he'd devised, his father would side check and edit them and then David would go visit Josh or spend the rest of the day at the Touro law library researching similar lawsuits to his and learning what he could and couldn't do legally in his own suit. Some afternoons he'd just take off and go to Atlantic City or Foxwoods.

One morning two weeks later David overheard the mailman chatting with the receptionist in the front as he dropped off the day's mail. A few minutes later his father came into the back room holding up a typed letter and an open envelope.

"I heard back from the Chancellor's office today," he said.

"About what?"

"I didn't tell you, but I wrote a letter to the Chancellor himself a couple weeks ago after Stefanik said you weren't cleared to teach yet because of our lawsuit."

""Really! What'd you say?

"I was thinking about what Judge Foster had said to that clown from the Board of Ed. Something like, 'if you don't get your heads together and resolve this, you're going to have a public relations nightmare on your hands.' Remember? I decided I was going to explain to the Chancellor just what kind of public relations nightmare he was going to have. I wrote him a twenty page letter detailing all the harassment and retaliatory actions they've taken against you. I just heard back from his lawyer today."

He held the letter high in the air, a satisfied look on his face.

"What did he say?" David asked.

"He threatened us."

"What?" Why did his father look so happy, David wondered.

"He warned me that any further communication from me to the Chancellor's office would violate the State Code of Ethics and that I'd be referred to the State Character and fitness Committee."

"What? Are you in trouble?"

"It's bullshit, just an empty threat, just more harassment."

"But what does it mean?"

"It means we're doing everything right."

CHAPTER 10

David brought Uncle Jeffrey with him to the grievance arbitration as his personal bodyguard. Uncle Jeffrey was a black belt in one of the martial arts – David wasn't sure which one – and David wanted him there for protection in case one of the weasels started something. David was forbidden to have his own lawyer with him at the proceeding.

He and Uncle Jeffrey sat on the wood bench in the hallway of the District Office outside the conference room they'd been assigned. Albert Morrison, the arbitrator, and John Scarpelli, the head of the Grievance Department for the union, had already arrived and were preparing themselves at the conference table in the room behind David and his uncle.

At issue was David's grievance against Harrison's and Schneider's letters that he'd claimed were not factual, and therefore unfair, and should be removed from his personnel file.

There was still ten minutes until the hearing had been scheduled to start and David was nervous that his new union advocate, Ms. Whitehall, would not arrive in time for them to talk before the proceeding. David fidgeted on the bench, only half paying attention to Uncle Jeffrey's chit-chat about his kids and about Michelle's new baby, until he heard high heels coming down the hall and saw Ms. Whitehall, dressed in a smart black suit, walking toward him, her hand already extended to him while she was still five feet away.

"Good morning, David. Let me brief you quickly on what will happen," she said and nodded to Uncle Jeffrey without showing any sign she wanted to be introduced to him. She sat down next to David. "We can only argue the unfairness of the letters, not their factual content. We'll bring up the outlandishness of the inferences, the uninvestigated claims and the lack of specifics. That's it. Okay?"

David nodded his head. He was more than happy to have Ms. Whitehall, in all her efficiency, handle everything once they went inside the conference room.

"Now, the best case scenario this morning is that the arbitrator suggests that the Union and the Board of Ed. work out some compromise before the grievance ever has to be sent up to the Office of Appeals and Reviews. You know, agree to delete some portions of the file while leaving others intact."

Wait a minute, David thought, as he began to wonder if the Union and the Board might actually collude to delete some of the unfair parts of the letters while leaving in just enough of the other unfair parts for the Office of Appeals and Reviews to maintain his Unsatisfactory rating down the road.

If they did, what could he do about it? The meeting was about to begin.

"Let me handle everything," Ms. Whitehall said and motioned for David to follow her into the room.

David obeyed. What choice did he have, he thought.

Ms. Whitehall walked over to the chair at the end of the conference table, sat down, opened her attaché case and pulled out a yellow pad and a stack of paperwork.

"Good morning, gentlemen," she said to the arbitrator and the union rep who were sitting on the far side of the long table. David sat to her right, facing the other two men.

"We're waiting for Ms. Harrison, Mr. Schneider and their advocate to arrive. Apparently they're running late," Morrison said, glancing down at his watch.

Twenty minutes of silence later, the three of them arrived, without apology, and sat in a row to David's right at the long table. It had been almost a year since David had seen either Harrison or Schneider, but he couldn't look them in the face, as he wanted to. They too sat facing Morrison and Scarpelli across the table. Their advocate sat between them. David could smell the heavy fragrance of Harrison's perfume even though she was sitting at the far end of the table from.

"Ms. Whitehall, you may begin," Morrison said.

Ms. Whitehall went over the unfairness of the letters without challenging the "observations" of Harrison or Schneider. She went over the inferences, exaggerations and lack of corroborating evidence presented in great detail, line by line in each letter, until she'd turned over each piece of paper in the pile of front of her and made a second pile, upside down, next to it.

Morrison started off by asking Schneider where the supporting evidence was that he had promised for David's "unescorted class" accusation.

"I was not able to present it at the Step One grievance hearing," he said.

"Given the immediacy to the incident of the date here on your letter, then, you apparently did no investigation. Is that right?" Morrison asked him.

"There's none presented here, no," Schneider said.

"Well, we can't have that," Morrison said. "Now, Ms. Harrison, what exactly is this letter of yours? An observation? A critique?"

"It's an observation. And a critique, Mr. Morrison."

"It has to be one or the other."

"Ms. Harrison, you're going to have to decide which one it is, for our purposes here," John Scarpelli, the Board advocate, said.

"Well, it was an informal observation."

"An 'informal' observation?" Morrison asked. "Then what's it doing here?"

"Well, it was really more of a formal observation. Yes, that's what it was. A formal observation, Mr. Morrison."

"Surely, principal, you must know not only the difference between a formal and an informal observation, but also to what use you can put each. Only a formal observation can be entered into a staff personnel file. I would have thought that was a rule you'd be quite familiar with at this point in your career, Ms. Harrison, no?"

"Of course I am. That particular letter…" Ms. Harrison began.

Morrison interrupted her to continue his lecture to her about the appropriate content of a personnel file and, when he was done, he asked Harrison, Schneider and David to leave the room for a few minutes.

David followed the two of them out into the hallway. He expected Harrison and Schneider to huddle together in muffled conversation, but Harrison walked to the other end of the bench and stood by herself while Schneider walked across the hallway and began examining the postings on a bulletin board hanging on the wainscoted wall of the old building.

David stood by the conference room door, wondering if they'd prearranged this separation, or if they were angry with each other now.

Uncle Jeffrey stayed sitting on the bench, but looked up at David to see how it was going. David made a show of shrugging his shoulders, but then threw his thumb into the air quickly, before Schneider or Harrison could see it.

Scarpelli came out shortly and called them all back into the room. After they'd seated themselves in a row on the near side of the table, Morrison again elaborated on what was appropriate to a personnel file, what they should do in that regard in the future and who they could contact if they needed advice on submitting their observations.

Good. He's admonishing them for breaking the rules of the game, David thought, the rules of their own game.

When Morrison had finished, Schneider raised a finger to speak. Morrison told him to go ahead.

"I'd like to submit this photocopy of a newspaper article to our proceedings today. It goes to the letters."

David saw the bold letters of the headline across the top of the photocopy as Schneider passed it over to Morrison. "Teacher Arrested."

"May we see that, please, sir?" Ms. Whitehall said.

Morrison read through the four paragraph article and then handed the shiny grey and white photocopy to Ms. Whitehall. She slid her chair over toward David and, their heads together, they both read the article silently.

David's face flushed bright red. He'd never known an article had appeared in the New York Daily News, under the Police Blotter section, the day after his arrest the previous June. It alleged that he had been arrested and charged with assault after the victim, another teacher at the school, claimed an injury caused by a pencil thrust into her back. The injury caused pain and a bruise, but the victim refused medical attention, the article said.

My name's smeared now, for millions to see, David thought. Sure, that was more fodder for the court case, given the damage to his reputation, he thought, but the fact was that his reputation really had been damaged. Irreparably. Everybody knew he was a criminal because the New York Daily News had said so. David was afraid he was going to cry.

It was too late for him to rebut it through the newspaper. And if that had failed, he couldn't even make a counter claim in his blog now. It was all too late. It's already out there that this is who I am.

One, two, three, four, five, six, seven.

"Let me see that, please," John Scarpelli said.

Ms. Whitehall slid the photocopy across the table to Scarpelli and pushed her chair back toward the end of the table. She looked at David, but for the moment she remained silent.

Scarpelli read quickly through the article and handed it angrily back to Morrison.

"Mr. Schneider, you're one disgusting man," Scarpelli said. "How dare you try Mr. Weintraub in the papers to start with, at the time of the incident, and how dare you now try to present this trash to the hearing to try to justify your own inept and ill minded letters about Weintraub. You're just…despicable."

"Listen, you weanie," Schneider yelled across the table to Scarpelli, "you have no right to talk to me like that. I have no idea how that article appeared in the paper. I had nothing to do with it, believe me, but it is an article in the city's press and it does state what it states and it's additional evidence about Mr. Weintraub's reputation and competence. Just look at him."

Schneider pointed over at David, who had been holding on to the edge of the table, trying to remain calm, trying not to cry, but now David looked at Schneider with eyes that showed an anger that Morrison thought would turn violent at any minute, and Weintraub was a big guy.

Scarpelli had already stood and was making his way around the table toward Schneider.

"That's it!" Morrison yelled. "Everyone back out in the hallway. Whitehall, Weintraub, you stay. Everyone else -- all of you children -- I'm giving you a time out, for chrissakes! Actually, Mr. Schneider, Dr. Harrison, I'm done with you for the day. You can go. Scarpelli, do you think you can behave yourself now?'

David wished he had his mother's leather harness to give to Morrison so he could strap Schneider to the iron radiator on the wall behind him.

"Yes, I can, sir," Scarpelli said quietly and went and sat back down in his chair.

Schneider and Harrison stood up and rushed out of the room together, Schneider pushing Harrison through the doorway with his hand flat across her lower back.

"We just can't have that," Morrison said. "Good heavens." He shook his head, partially in disgust, partially to shake the dizzying commotion of the last few minutes out of it. "Ms. Whitehall, Mr. Weintraub, give me a second here to confer with Mr. Scarpelli."

David watched Morrison and Scarpelli lean toward each other and quietly, too quietly for David to hear, discuss what should be done. After several minutes of back and forth and nodding, Morrison turned back to David.

"Mr. Weintraub, we are removing Mr. Schneider's letter from your file altogether and deleting paragraphs two through six of Ms. Harrison's letter. That leaves, from her letter, 'I observed your classroom covered with garbage indicating your failure to maintain proper student discipline and classroom management. If you don't improve, you will be subject to an unsatisfactory rating.' You're now free to request the removal of your Unsatisfactory rating from the Office of Appeals and Review. We're done here today. I thank you. Thank you for your presence, as well – your calm, well behaved presence -- Ms. Whitehall."

The four of them stood and filed out of the room.

"Got a little noisy in there, huh?" Uncle Jeffrey said to David after he came out into the hallway. "Didn't know if I should come in or not. Was there a fight?"

"It was close."

"How'd you make out?"

"I was accused of having garbage on my floor."

"Garbage? What's that mean?"

"It means that neither the union nor the bureaucrat weasels have any sense of justice or mercy. They have to accuse me of something.'

"Sounds like everybody's out to get you."

"Sounds like it."

David wished he could calm down, but he kept feeling his arms and hands shaking. He just wanted a Cherry Cola. A large Cherry Cola.

He and his uncle walked slowly down the granite steps at the front of the building, turned left on the sidewalk and made their way through the lunch hour crowd walking towards them. Secretaries who had changed into their sneaks for lunchtime exercise, men in crisp shirts and ties under their open spring jackets, and teenage Latino boys, all in black jeans and hoodies, made their way past David and his uncle.

David looked into the face of each person who passed him and tried to tell if they recognized him. Had they read that Daily News article? Did they recognize him just from his height and weight, both mentioned in the piece? Did everyone know who he was, the teacher who'd assaulted a fellow teacher? That's what the Daily News had said.

One businessman stared back at David, eye to eye, challenging him, as the two of them passed each other on the sidewalk, and several women turned their heads from his direct gaze after they saw him staring at them. David didn't know if they were avoiding him because he was staring at them, or because of his size, or because they knew he was the teacher they'd read about in the paper. He'd stabbed someone.

He wished he could be invisible.

One, two, three, four, five, six, seven.

Both Santini and Stefanik kept stalling about allowing David to go back into the classroom, each passing the buck to the other, until they finally both agreed that it was up to "legal" down at the Board of Ed. to clear him.

Yes, they said, it was all "legal's" fault.

David wanted to teach, and if they weren't going to put him back with Doug Fisher, he'd see if he could be placed elsewhere, maybe in another district where they hadn't heard of him yet. There was a job fair coming up in early May, but he decided to make some phone calls first to see what his "status" was in the system before he arrived at that fair. He didn't want any alarms going off loudly in the middle of the gymnasium when they plugged his name into the computer there.

First he called the office of the Executive Director of Human Resources Office in charge of Personnel Investigations.

"I'm sorry, Mr. Weintraub, but you're ineligible to teach in a New York City school, sir. You've been discontinued," the secretary told him after he'd asked her to look up his status in the computer.

"I'm not eligible to teach in another district?" David asked.

"No, sir. You were discontinued for some reason. Do you know why?"

"I was given an Unsatisfactory rating from a prior district."

"You can resubmit your resume, but at the moment you're ineligible to work in any district."

"Thank you, ma'am."

Next David called the Teachers Monitoring Unit at the New York Board of Ed.

After being transferred to four different staff, David finally reached a woman who said she could help him.

"I need to know what I need to do to remove myself from the 'Ineligible to Teach' list, please," he said.

There was a minute of silence on the other end while she scrolled up his name on the computer in front of her.

"You're not on the ineligible list, sir."

"Personnel said I was ineligible."

"Well, you're not on that list here."

"Can you transfer me back to Personnel?"

A Mr. Henderson picked up and introduced himself at the Personnel office.

"I want to check why I'm on your ineligible list," David said to him.

A minute of silence.

"Sir, you're eligible. I don't see anything wrong here. You were cleared in the system last December twenty-third."

"Are you sure?" David asked, irritated, but trying to remain calm. After all, Mr. Henderson now knew that David had been arrested for assault. It was right on the computer screen in front of him, just like being in the paper. What was Henderson thinking about him?

"We investigated the arrest," Henderson said, "evaluated your situation and finally cleared you in the system last December."

"Thank you, Mr. Henderson."

David hung up the phone and wondered what exactly all that meant, but he decided it was worth a chance to go to the job fair and, like playing his odds against a bad draw in poker, applying for a job teaching for the next fall. It was going to depend what computer screen in what office they looked at if he was blackballed or not.

Actually, David thought, it was more like Russian roulette than poker.

David arrived at the Board of Ed. job fair that May in the same gymnasium with the same tables and the same uncomfortable little folding metal chairs. He sat, observed and chose his mark after he'd identified the least serious, least bureaucratic-looking group of school employees. They were from a school in another notoriously rough South Bronx district.

The staff developer, Ms. Gonzalez according to her name tag, a young woman with long, straight hair, immediately offered him a fifth grade position, but he would have to talk to Hal Smirnov, the principal, to confirm his acceptance. Smirnov had an opening for an interview the next Monday. How was that?

David accepted and listened to the woman fill him in, as diplomatically as she could, about the neighborhood, measuring his response, it seemed, to the type of children he'd be dealing with. David let her know his background in Bushwick and the Bronx, and she said, "Okay, then, no worries. You know what I'm talking about."

As he left the gymnasium, David was more worried about how long his job offer might last than about having to deal with more rough street kids. They hadn't plugged his name into the computer at the table at the far end of the gymnasium, just said he should show up for the meeting with Smirnov, but David was anxious about what might happen when someone did enter his name. Would he even make into a classroom on the first day? And if he did, how long would it be before one of those weasels began screwing with him again, once they found out who he was.

He just wanted to teach. He loved teaching, and if this was what he had to do to teach, so be it, he thought. I'm going to get these guys in the end anyway.

When David got home, he called Lisa Petrocelli to see if she could find out anything for him about Hal Smirnov before he went to meet him. She called him back later that afternoon.

"Smirnov was kicked out of P.S. 62 about fifteen years ago because of his abusive character. Not only to the kids, but to the other teachers and the administrators. Like your friend, Nelson, he spent almost five years cooling his heels and twiddling his thumbs in the district offices. He only got himself a position – originally in an assistant principal spot – because of a union technicality. Be careful of him, David."

"I'm careful of everybody."

"I'm still rubbing my top hat for you," Lisa said.

Hal Smirnov came out of his office to meet David only a few minutes after David had announced himself to his secretary. He was in his late fifties and had a paunch that stretched his white shirt across the front of him so much that the shirt buckled between its lower buttons. David thought there was an old food stain on one side which must never have washed out completely in the laundry.

He looked like a guy who liked his turkey grinders with sautéed peppers, David thought, so maybe he wouldn't be all that bad.

"So how come you're not working at P.S. 67, Weintraub?" Smirnov asked.

No hello, no how are you, just a challenge. Oh, boy, David thought.

"It's kind of a long story, sir," David said. "Basically, there was a mistake made downtown, but it's been all cleared up now. Mostly all cleared up, that is."

David realized he didn't have the courage to tell Smirnov everything that had happened. This was the first time he had had to talk to a stranger about it, and he was too uncomfortable, too embarrassed, to bring up the arrests for inappropriate physical behavior or for assault, even though all those charges had now been thrown out.

He had been labeled in the school system, and in the New York Daily News, and even if all the charges had been dropped, he still felt the social stigma, still felt he had a scarlet U on his forehead for anybody, including Hal Smirnov, to see.

He didn't know if he would ever get over that.

"I've had my troubles with downtown myself," Smirnov said, snorting some air out through his puffy lips. "Let me give you a quick tour, show you what'll be your classroom in the fall. Fifth grade, unruliest section to start. I hear you have experience."

"Yes. Yes, I do."

David walked side by side with Smirnov through the halls, peeking into offices and classrooms, and David became aware that no one seemed at all comfortable around the principal. The teachers and office staff gave timid "hello, sir's" and some actually looked nervous, maybe even frightened, when Smirnov entered their offices or their classrooms. The kids who poured out into the hallways during one lunch break all looked the other way when they saw him. Not one child greeted him and he didn't say a word to any of them.

After they'd completed their tour of the old brick building, Smirnov stood with David in the hall by the front doors and told him he'd call him the following Monday to let him know if he'd be able to teach there.

David felt lousy all the way on his long drive home, but he knew at least he might be able to teach that next fall, and once he got into his classroom and shut the door, he could create his own world with his kids, no matter what was happening in this other world outside.

Smirnov called him first thing the following Monday morning.

"David, I called Doug Fisher over at 67. They think the world of you over there," Smirnov said.

"Yes, sir."

"To be honest with you, I was having a bit of a bad day last Monday. Sorry. Fisher told me what was happening with your court cases and stuff. That's bullshit. I'm going to put you on the roster for the fall. My secretary will call you with the details."

"Thank, you, Mr. Smirnov," David said, but Smirnov had already hung up.

David thought he had sounded like he was having another "bit of a bad day" today, too. Maybe Mondays were kind of rough on him. Something seemed not quite right with Smirnov, but David was happy to be able to teach again. And to make some money again. He had a lot of bills to pay.

The little conference room was crowded at David's final grievance arbitration for his Unsatisfactory rating.

David and his union advocate, Mark Feinberg, sat huddled together at one end of the long conference table. To their right sat Schneider, Harrison, Menendez and the district director, Frank Waltrip. To David's left, facing the four defendants, sat the three members of the Appeals and Review Board, the chairman Jacob Cooper, from the Union, Bob Hutchinson, the Chancellor's Office rep, and Myra Spangenberg, a former principal and supposedly unbiased third member of the board. She drummed her glossy white fingernails on the polished wood surface of the conference table, quietly, but enough to make her presence known.

David was suspicious of her. He had heard from Feinberg that Spangenberg had often sided with the administration and against the union at a number of the boards she had been appointed to. "We'll need to watch out for her," he'd said.

Feinberg was the first to speak and he immediately asked for a dismissal of the Unsatisfactory rating.

"There's nothing left in Mr. Weintraub's file other than a mundane comment about some garbage. I have asked Ms. Harrison on two occasions to elaborate on what's left of her report in the file, but she has never responded."

"I didn't know who was on the phone, so of course I wasn't going to respond to an unidentified request for more information," Harrison said.

David and Feinberg both knew he had identified himself on the phone, both times by name and as a representative of the union working on the grievance.

"I'd like to request a brief recess while I speak with the district Director, Mr. Waltrip," Myra Spangenberg suddenly announced.

Jacob Cooper, the Board chairman, nodded.

"You know," Feinberg leaned over and whispered to David, "at this point the other side would normally drop this. Anybody with a brain would run for the hills right now and just try to minimize the damage."

"You don't know these guys as well as I do, Mark," David whispered back. "They have no brains."

After several minutes, Spangenberg and Waltrip returned to their seat and Waltrip spoke.

"I recommend that Mr. Feinberg's request to drop the Unsatisfactory rating be taken under advisement at this point and that we proceed."

The three board members looked at each other and then nodded okay.

See no evil, hear no evil, speak no evil, David thought, as he looked at the three of them. The two clear plastic reels spinning on the top of the tape recorder at the other end of the table caught his eye. Too bad it couldn't record these puppet's heads nodding.

Feinberg passed a copy of Chancellor's regulation 456 to each person at the table. It stated that in order to rate someone Unsatisfactory for the year, there had to be two, full period observation reports in the teacher's file.

"As you know," he said, "there is not even one full period observation report in Mr. Weintraub's file. Can we please dismiss this U rating?"

"Mr. Feinberg," Menendez said, "your point is understood, but there is a concern in the district for the welfare of the children if Mr. Weintraub returns to the class room. You know, given all of his previous inappropriate behavior."

"That's right," Harrison added. "You know there's still a restraining order against Mr. Wientraub from one of the teachers, Ms. Fontagne, I believe."

Feinberg turned to look at David. David shook his head "no."

"The fact is," Harrison continued, ignoring David's denial, "Weintraub has been remanded to the district office because of the allegations of corporal punishment. If that isn't grounds for an Unsatisfactory rating of a teacher, what is?"

"Mr. Chairman, I'd like to request another brief break," Spangenberg said.

"Alright," Cooper said. David could tell he was not happy when he saw Waltrip rise again and accompany Spangenberg outside into the hallway.

When they returned, the chairman addressed David.

"Mr. Weintraub, may I ask you, please, to tell us all your side of these events."

139

David took a moment to steel himself before he spoke. Several nasty comments and several catty jokes had come to his mind immediately, but he took a deep breath and spoke slowly. Feinberg had had him practice his short speech many times that morning, until he was satisfied David could deliver it verbatim, flawlessly and calmly.

"I am a good educator. After a series of false allegations from these administrators, there is virtually nothing left in my file other than a comment, also incorrect, about some garbage on my classroom floor one day. I therefore respectfully request that the Unsatisfactory rating be overturned so I can get on with my life and be able to teach elsewhere without further harassment next fall."

"Is that all you wish to say?" Cooper asked.

"What else is there to say?" David shot out. "This isn't complicated."

"Alright, then," the chairman said. "Now, do any of you wish to cross examine Mr. Weintraub?"

"Mr. Chairman?" Spangenberg interrupted. "One more brief recess please?"

"This is your last one, Myra. But go ahead," Cooper told her.

After she and Waltrip had returned again, Vice Principal Schneider spoke.

"I have a question for Mr. Weintraub. How is it that you reported you had the 'highest' reading group when, in fact, you had the lowest fifth grade class?"

Is this the best argument against me you can come up with, David thought. What a loser.

"Sir," David answered, "of the four monolingual reading groups, I had the second highest. Ms. Harrison herself -- at the 1998 faculty conference meeting, remember? -- was the one who reported that the fifth grade in our school was the only one to do well in the reading proficiency tests. Every child in my class reached the standards for the practice test at that time."

"Mr. Weintraub," Principal Harrison broke in, "how is it that despite all of the demonstration lessons given by the staff developer, you still did not improve as a teacher?"

"Just how far below the belt is this woman willing to hit?" David whispered to Feinberg as he pondered his best response to her accusation. He noticed that today was the first time he had ever seen her without a string of beads looped around her neck. She had nothing to fondle. "Next thing you know, Mark, she's going to be accusing me of causing 9/11, global warming and worldwide poverty."

"Calm down, David," Feinberg whispered back.

"Mr. Weintraub? Do you wish to respond?" Cooper asked.

"All the new teachers," David said, "were given demonstration lessons about once a week, Ms. Harrison. I received no more and no less than any other new teacher and improved no more and no less than any of the other new teachers. I might also point out that the staff developer had written a letter, which somehow never made it into my file, refuting your claim about there being garbage on my floor the day you said there was. That was one of the days she was in my classroom giving a demonstration.'

The chairman was about to speak when Waltrip now interrupted, talking loudly.

"Mr. Weintraub, are you suggesting then that everything here has been fabricated? I also would like to know if you feel you have any deficiencies, any deficiencies at all, as a teacher?"

"Yes, indeed," David said. "Everything has been fabricated. And although I am a satisfactory teacher, like every other teacher in America, there is always room for improvement."

There was silence in the room until Myra Spangenberg started tapping her nails on the table again.

"Alright then," Chairman Cooper said. "I don't think there is anything else that we need to go over here today, is there?"

No one spoke.

"Then this Appeals and review Board hearing is over. Mr. Weintraub, we will notify you in writing of our decision. Thank you, everyone."

David didn't think Cooper looked at all happy at how things had gone, but David was still not the least bit sure that Cooper had David's best interests at heart.

As David and Feinberg walked out into the hallway, David saw Spangenberg pull Waltrip over to the far wall and the two of them started talking to each other. From across the hallway David couldn't tell if they were excited about what had just happened or if they were just angry at each other.

He also wondered what they were planning for him next.

Three weeks later David had still not heard from the Board. He called the Appeals and Review office. The secretary claimed they were backlogged, but that the decision had been sent over to Human resources for "editing." Once it came back from HR, she told him, it would be sent on to the Chancellor's Office for final approval and signature. Once they received it back, they'd forward him a copy.

Three more weeks passed with no response from the Board.

David told his father and his father called a lawyer he knew who did occasional work for the Chancellor's office and asked him for a favor. Two days later David read a copy of the determination which the lawyer had made for David's father.

"Mr. Weintraub said he was a good teacher, "…but nobody was perfect. You learn on the way. There is nothing in my file. Therefore, my record is clean." He expressed his willingness to go elsewhere because he loves to teach and wants to help the children of New York. Mr. Weintraub wants his record clean and, furthermore, he feels he deserves an "S" rating.

There was no documentation to substantiate anything.

The Board unanimously feels compelled, based on the complete lack of any evidence or documentation, not to concur with the recommendation to discontinue Mr. Weintraub's probationary service."

As David read through the final lines of the finding, he was startled to find there were tears in his eyes.

Maybe the *whole* world wasn't against him.

CHAPTER 11

That summer David was happy.

His criminal charges had been thrown out, his Unsatisfactory rating had been overturned, and nothing seemed as serious to him as it had. He was beating them at their own game. He was Ghandi.

The more he thought about it, driving down to Bally's casino or up to the Touro law library, the more he began to consider himself a Tai Chi master, turning the weasel bureaucrat's own negative energy right back against them so they'd actually end up defeating themselves. Maybe Ghandi had learned his tricks from those Asians too. Maybe, David thought, he should turn his attention away from chess and take up Go.

He felt, the more he studied law, that he was playing a higher level of game, a level where the rules of the game itself were refined and then kept in, not a level where everyone was using force and cruelty to see how many of the rules they could break for their own selfish purposes, a level where the little guy always got crushed by the most base of human attributes.

Law was a higher level game. Law protected the little guy.

Funny that the law had been right under his nose all the time he was growing up, with an attorney for a father, and yet he had never seen the importance of it, or the appeal of it. It was almost better than math. One, two, three, four, five, six, seven.

That summer he spent many evenings hunched over his keyboard typing out blog after blog on his "davefromqueens" page and arguing populist, progressive politics with a host of other would-be politicians on his and on a number of other on-line public forums. He developed a stream of ardent supporters – he called them his "cyber groupies" -- and an almost equally vociferous stream of ardent opponents, and he loved it all.

At one point he thought about running against his Republican state senator in the next election and he started writing press releases and position statements for himself under his new political moniker, Big davefromqueens. After all, if he were elected to the state senate, he would be a legislator, an actual designer of the laws that protected the little guy in the state of New York. He'd be legislating the rules of the game that everybody, and particularly the state's educators, would have to play by. It would be perfect.

With his sister Karen's invitations, he also started attending singles groups, looking for the perfect woman. At first he loved showing attractive women his skills at instantaneously memorizing their phone numbers or adding up in his head multi-digit numbers, but none of the women he met seemed to him to be appropriately impressed with that, so he started talking politics with them. He found that was not successful either. By the middle of the summer he was listing for the women he met the qualities he was most attracted to in a woman -- intelligence, integrity, potential as a mother, sense of humor -- complete with his numerical rankings for each category, but by August he still had not landed a date.

At the casinos he was far more successful. The female dealers loved his joking with them, they laughed at his funny faces, and he could tell they admired him for the fact that he almost always had won at the poker table by the end of the day -- often just a little, and seldom a huge amount, but almost always a win. He tipped them well. After all, they too were "little guys." But he never asked one of them for a date.

He spent hours of research at the Touro law library, always in his one favorite swivel chair in a carrel at the far back corner of the large main study room. At first he worked mostly on studying the art of turning the answers from the depositions his father was taking into ammunition for the salvos they would need for their eventual questioning of the weasels in the court room.

Soon, though, he was researching First Amendment cases and the precedents that had been set as he began gathering what his father needed so he could put together his own First Amendment violation case for the United States Second Circuit Court. If he and his father could prove that David's freedom of speech rights had been violated by his employers, a new level of protection would be afforded any worker, anywhere in the country, from the kind of oppressive treatment he had received from the New York weasels.

On the afternoons he didn't go to the Atlantic City or Foxwoods casinos, he'd drive to his father's office after he finished at the Touro law library and study the most recent batch of depositions his father had taken. He'd found a little Jewish deli about three blocks from his father's office that had the thickest, juiciest hot pastrami he'd ever had, and a mound of that on a Kaiser roll with plenty of sauerkraut and mustard, oozing out the sides, had replaced his turkey grinders as lunch. They had Cherry Cola at the deli too. He'd always buy two cans.

As much as he could, he would "hang out," as he put it, with his newest nephew, Jonathon, propped up under his arm on the family room sofa at Michelle's, watching movies.

He was happy.

One afternoon he drove into Brooklyn to his old school in Bushwick to see Lisa and share all his good news with her. As he sat in bumper to bumper traffic, he pictured the smile on her face when he told her they'd been victorious. She was so sweet. Maybe she'd even give him a hug.

He rapped his secret knock on the dark wood of her office door and slowly pushed it open, even before he heard her answer. He stuck his face around the edge of the door, his best smile carefully displayed, and stopped.

A young man with blond hair stood up from behind Lisa's desk.

"Can I help you?" he asked.

"Where's Lisa," David asked. Maybe she's sick today, he thought, or on vacation. This guy's her fill-in.

"Lisa Petrocelli? Oh, she moved to Atlanta a couple weeks ago. I'm her replacement. John Hodges." The young man walked around the desk with his hand out.

"Atlanta? Why Atlanta?"

"That's where her fiancée lives."

"Fiancée?"

"Yeah. You know, what was his name, Simpson."

"Oh, right. Simpson. Of course."

Hodges took another step forward, his hand still out in front of him, but David quietly pulled the office door shut and walked down the hall toward the front stairs.

The last time I went down these stairs, David remembered, was when Freddie Donnelly had me in those handcuffs. That wasn't as painful as today.

One afternoon a week later David was sitting at the conference table in the back room of his father's offices with the transcripts of the depositions his father had taken spread out in front of him in neat piles. As he read through the testimony of each, he made notes on a fresh yellow legal pad in front of him.

"These guys are just unbelievable!" he finally yelled over his shoulder toward the doorway behind him when he heard his father coming down the hall.

"They've all got the 'don't recall disease,' that's for sure," his dad said

145

as he walked up behind David and placed his hand on his son's shoulder.

"Harrison just lies, time after time, when she says anything other than 'I don't really remember.' Only once does she break down and finally admit she had a meeting with Menendez. You know, when he'd showed her our notice of claim to sue them. That'll be one of our collusion points, for sure. Otherwise, she just tries to pin everything on Schneider."

"And when I deposed him, he tried to pin everything on her. What a pair."

"When you asked him if he had kept notes about his meetings, he said 'Yes,' but then he lets it drop that all those notes had been stolen the second week of June. Mighty convenient theft, eh? He probably hired Jesus to do it."

"Yeah, but as long as they're equally as evasive on the witness stand, they'll show themselves as the fools they are."

"Worse than fools. You know, when I was in jail that night, at least the criminals there admitted what they'd done. They may not have felt much guilt, but at least they fessed up to what they'd done. These guys aren't even up to admitting what they did. Morally, they're worse than street criminals. Unbelievable."

"Their counsel is going to drag this thing out for as many years as they can, you know. Have you thought of settling out of court?"

"I'm never backing off. As you once said to me, I want to 'hold their feet to the fire.' Their smelly, ugly, cloven feet. Do weasels have cloven feet?"

"These do," his dad said and patted David on his shoulder before he turned and went back to his own office.

David picked up the deposition of Freddie Donnelly, the school safety guard who'd arrested him for stabbing Ms. Fontagne. David chuckled as he read Freddie's continued insistence that he himself was the one who had decided to arrest David, even though it had been obvious to David at the time that the two New York City policemen weren't sure they wanted to have anything to do with the matter and had used Freddie to do their dirty work for him.

Poor Freddie, a little guy, David realized, still trying to ensure he's given credit for what would be his only fifteen minutes of fame, ever. He'd never have another chance to actually arrest anyone, and he probably had no clue that he might not ever have the authority, as seen by the courts, to arrest anybody, let alone somebody for whom there was no probable cause for the arrest.

David re-read the section where his father had kept asking Freddie if there was probable cause. Freddie'd answered that of course there was, Ms. Fontagne had said so. Directly to Freddie? Well, no. Did Schneider say so? Well, no. Did he see any evidence of a stab wound? Well, no. David realized

Freddie didn't even know exactly what 'probable cause' meant.

Suddenly David started laughing uncontrollably. The absurdity of the entire incident finally hit him. Stabbed with a pencil, but no hole in the dress, no wound or bruise to be seen by anyone, Harrison and Schneider each trying to pass the buck to the other about who first heard of the 'stabbing,' who then called 911, who told the police what happened, who had a direct report from Ms. Fontagne and, David remembered, Ms. Fontagne herself standing there, peacock head peeking out the neck of her dress with its tiny eyes observing the buffoonery around her. And Freddie, standing there, proud as punch.

Not that it had seemed buffoonery to David then, but right now the whole scene struck him as impossibly funny.

"You alright in there?" he heard his father call out down the hallway.

"Just fine, dad. Just fine," he called back and wiped the tears of laughter from his cheeks.

Once he settled down, David continued to read Freddie's deposition. Freddie had balked when he was asked a second time if it hadn't been the NYPD who had told him to arrest David, and he asserted his pride again at it being his decision.

David felt sorry for Freddie. Here was an innocent little guy, probably trying to support a wife and a couple kids the best way he knew how, too naive to really know if what he was doing was even legal, let alone right, far too carried away with the understandable satisfaction he was feeling to be able to see that Harrison and Schneider and Fontagne had probably cooked up the whole incident just to nail David. Freddie was being taken advantage of.

When he finally appeared in court, on the stand, he'd be made mince meat of, the poor guy. He wasn't even the target of the weasels' malice, but he'd be a victim of it nonetheless.   The system and the weasels running it contaminate everyone, David thought.

David read Fontagne's deposition next and saw that she, too, was a "little guy" and also contaminated by an authoritarian bureaucracy where evil minded men and women had the power to take advantage of others. Fontagne, like Freddie, was just trying to make a living, and to her, going along with Harrison's and Schneider's plot against David was a way to further her career. She'd probably had enough failures and losses already in her life, David realized, and so she decided to go along with their plot in hopes of future rewards.

David felt sorry for Freddie and Fontagne. They were just like him. Little guys.

Well, he thought, he at least felt sorry for Freddie. For Fontagne, maybe not so much. She had something in her that would have made her a full fledged weasel herself, David could see, if she had ever gotten into a position of authority, like Harrison and Schneider had.

She was contaminated too. Maybe all that ink from her peacock tattoo had finally damaged her brain. David laughed to himself. I guess I feel a little sorry for her.

When he started teaching again in late August, David gave up any thought of making a bid for the local state senator seat. All his evenings were spent preparing for class, his days commuting and teaching, and his weekends at the casinos earning the extra money he needed to get out of the debt he'd accumulated from not having any teacher income that year.

He practiced new card tricks to help his fifth grade students learn math and observation, he developed a funny routine about "stuff" and "energy" to explain nouns and verbs to them, and he put together a clever question and answer game to teach them world geography. He loved it.

The kids in his fifth grade class had never seen anything like him and within a few weeks most of them were engaged in learning for the first time in their lives. He had two or three rough street boys, but he realized, thankfully, there was not one Jesus in his classroom.

Principal Smirnov was giving David free reign, and neither he nor either of the vice principals showed up to "observe" David's teaching. The school's staff developer, so young David at first thought she was an interning college sophomore, would come once a week and try to offer David the standard educational tips, but it soon became apparent to her that David knew far better than she how to engage and handle the kids. She'd arrive Friday mornings at ten, sit crunched into a desk in the last row of his classroom, her chin on her folded hands, and just enjoy watching him teach.

Outside his classroom, though, David still felt the aura of isolation among the staff which he'd noticed on his first tour with Smirnov earlier that summer. The culture of the school had been forged by Smirnov's own personality – this school is in the key of…David hummed "bump, bump, bump, bum" to himself – and while Smirnov didn't seem to be the menace of either a Harrison or a Schneider, he was not a comfortable man to be around. Over the years he too had been contaminated by the New York Board of Ed. bureaucratic cancer. He too was a weasel, even if not a very dangerous or powerful one.

That November David was asked to fill in one day for a teacher who had unexpectedly called in sick. Her class was one of the most unruly in the school and even though she could handle them as well as anyone, Smirnov assigned David to the class because the substitute who had first arrived earlier that morning was clearly not up to the task. Smirnov had switched her in David's classroom instead for the rest of the day.

"I know who you are!" one sixth grader yelled to David as soon as he entered the room.

"And who might I be?" David asked happily, thinking maybe the boy had heard how much David's own class liked him.

"You're the guy who stabbed some other teacher in Brooklyn," the boy said.

David stopped in the middle of the floor in front of the seated kids. He felt his heart flutter for a minute.

"Where did you hear that?"

"Well, aren't you?" the boy said and looked around at the rest of the students in the class for support.

"I asked you where you heard that," David said.

"From Mr. Wilson, one day, in the lunchroom."

David scanned the twenty or so faces looking up at him expectantly from their desks.

"Well, that was a lie. I never stabbed any teacher. I never even stabbed a student. I mean, can you believe it? You know how bad those students can be."

Two or three in the class laughed and a couple others giggled under their breath.

"Has anyone here ever had someone tell a lie about them?" David asked "You know, said something about you that made you get in trouble or just made you sound bad to your friends?"

Eleven hands immediately shot up into the air.

"You," David pointed to a girl in the front row, "tell me what happened."

He spent most of the next hour listening to each student tell his tale of being done wrong. Afterward he had them offer their opinions about why people lied to get others in trouble. The class liked him.

The rest of the day went smoothly, but as David drove home that afternoon he began to wonder if the dark aura of isolation he felt at school was not really the other teachers' and staff's reaction to Smirnov, as he had thought, but their reaction to David himself. Had they all heard, too, that he'd stabbed another teacher?

Was he now so stigmatized throughout the New York school system that he couldn't ever feel comfortable here, couldn't ever do well here? Was there any higher up he could trust in this system? Was there even any peer, any other teacher, he could befriend?

David's heart told him that he was a good teacher and that he needed to stick this out, he needed not to give up, but his head told him that he was going to be messed with again and again, one way or another, and the weasels would keep trying to destroy him no matter what.

He liked what he felt in his heart, but he was worried what was in his head was actually the truth.

In December Smirnov walked into David's classroom the afternoon before Christmas vacation. David's students had already left, and the principal, his face serious, went directly over to David, sitting at his desk and looking up at Smirnov, surprised.

Smirnov placed his hands, widely apart, on the surface of the desk and leaned up close to David's face.

"We know all about you from Brooklyn, you know," he said to David. "You better not come back here next year."

Smirnov pushed himself back up to a standing position, said "Know what I mean?" and turned and walked out of the room.

David knew what was in his head was, in fact, the truth.

Two days later a certified letter arrived at David's apartment.

> *Dear Mr. Weintraub:*
> *Please be advised that this will constitute your second and final notification.*
>
> *On July 28, 2000, I notified you regarding the reversal of my prior recommendation to Discontinue your Probationary Service. You were* instructed
> *to report to my office for assignment on September 5, 2000 at 9:30 a.m. To* date,
> *you have failed to appear and/or contact this office.*
>
> *If you do not report to the District Office within twenty days after receipt of* this
> *letter, it will be considered as abandonment of your position.*
>
> > *Very truly yours,*
> > *Ramon Menendez,*
> *Superintendent*

David sat on his sofa and read the letter through again. There had been no earlier letter. Menendez was setting David up for abandonment so he could terminate him once and for all.

David called his dad.

An hour later his father called him back and said he'd contacted the Board of Ed. lawyers and they'd agreed to contact Menendez and get him to back off from this obviously false accusation. David worried, though, that the damage had already been done because Smirnov would have been made aware of this letter, probably had even been sent a copy of it.

When David returned to school after the Christmas break, he knew he'd been right. Smirnov called him down to his office before he began teaching the first period.

"You're going to have to leave here, David, or I'm going to write you up just like they did in Brooklyn," Smirnov said. He sat behind his desk, tapping a pencil up and down on his blotter, while David stood in front of him like a schoolboy ready to receive his punishment.

David could tell by Smirnov's face that he was having another one of his "bad days."

"You got Menendez's letter, huh?"

"Look, David. I have my orders. It's you, so I have to do what I have to do."

David knew he was a sitting duck. Possibly a dead duck. There was no longer anyone in the system who wasn't going to take a shot at him. Either he'd be fired for some trumped up charge or – and he knew this was what they really wanted – he'd drop his lawsuit, or at least settle it quickly, and be gone from the New York City school system forever. Either way, they'd win.

He wasn't going to let them win.

He loved teaching. He wasn't going to give that up. But if he was fired by them, he'd never be able to teach in New York City again. Maybe not anywhere else either.

"I've got an idea," David said to Smirnov.

"Oh, yeah?"

"I'll resign, but just from your school. I'll write up a letter of resignation from here – with whatever iron clad terms you need to satisfy your own butt not getting into trouble – and then you'll give me a Satisfactory rating for the year and come June 22nd, I'm gone from here."

"That might work," Smirnov said, holding the pencil still in front of him. "But I'm going to put a couple letters in your file, suggesting your incompetence, just in case you reneg. When I get your letter of resignation, I'll pull them."

"Deal."

"Deal. Now go teach, and I don't want to talk to you again. At all. For the rest of the year."

After school that day David went back to his apartment, typed out his letter of resignation, signed it and put it into an envelope marked "Hal Smirnov, Principal." Principal weasel, David said to himself and slid the envelope into his briefcase to take to school with him the next morning.

Next he reached over and pulled the application papers for Touro Law School toward him. They had been sitting there on the back of his desk for six months, ever since he'd picked them up one afternoon after doing his research in the law library. He'd looked at them every time he sat down at his desk.

David clicked the button at the top of his ball point pen.

151

It was time to go to law school.

That spring the Board of Education lawyers continued with their endless stall tactics. When David's father requested a document from them that he had every right to request, they'd respond weeks later with a denial of the request because it was "too vague" or "not reasonably calculated." David's father would appeal their denial, it would go to a judge for adjudication and in every case, the documents would be provided. David knew that although weeks were being lost at the moment, months and even years of their legal stalling tactics were in his future.

If that's the way they wanted to play it, so be it. He wasn't giving up.

In May he went to the Board of Ed. job fair so that he could secure a position at a different school for the next year. There were still no teaching jobs open in Long Island. If he was going to teach, it seemed, for the moment it would have to be in New York City. He could do that and still start law school part-time.

He was sitting at one of the interview tables in the gymnasium talking to Mr. Zeller, the principal of P.S. 54, near 125th and Broadway in the Bronx, when a tall woman in a dark green skirt and jacket came over to them.

"I'm sorry to interrupt you, principal, but you should know that this man is U rated from Brooklyn. He's on the 'Do not hire list,'" she said.

"Is that true, Mr. Weintraub?" the Principal asked.

"Of course not."

"But Mrs. Wilson here is from the Chancellor's Office."

"That hardly surprises me," David said. "Big Brother is watching us. Or in this case, Big Sister."

Zeller looked from David back up into the tall woman's face. She raised an impatient eyebrow.

"Well," Zeller said, "I think we're going to have to end your interview. If I find out anything's different, I'll call you. I've got your number." He held up David's application papers.

"I think you all have my number," David said, stood, threw one of his practiced smiles at Big Sister and strolled out of the gymnasium.

He was done with New York.

He'd have to find somewhere else to teach, maybe in a private school, maybe as a tutor, but it was time to play a different game.

It was time to go to law school.

CHAPTER 12

One afternoon, seven years later, David's best friend Barry was sitting across from him at David's kitchen table, waiting for the pizza to arrive.

"David, are you sure you can do tomorrow afternoon too?" Barry asked.

"Sure. We'll do the rest of the tort stuff tonight after we eat and then I'll be home from teaching about noon tomorrow. Just come over about one."

Barry and David had met and become good friends in law school, even though David was two years ahead of Barry, and now Barry worked with David in David's dad's law offices. David had passed the bar three years earlier and now he was helping Barry prep for the bar exam that Barry would take in seven days.

David had started off being Barry's mentor in law school, even giving him some of his expensive law texts that he no longer needed and that Barry couldn't easily afford. David had done the same with some other lower classmen as well, but Barry and David had shared a passion for politics that had become a foundation for their friendship. Once David convinced his father to hire Barry as an interning attorney, they became even closer friends.

The buzzer to David's apartment rang, loud and long.

"Alright! Pizza!" David said.

"Great," Barry said. "My favorite comfort food."

"Barry, are you kidding? Every food is a comfort food."

David brought the large flat boxes and two tall drinks back to the kitchen table, pulled off a handful of napkins from the counter and put a paper plate in front of each of them.

"I'm always amazed you can eat as much as you do," David said.

Barry was short and skinny and his black curly hair was thinning even though he was only in his early thirties. He peered back at David through his wire frame glasses.

"I've got the metabolism of a shrew. If I don't eat five times my body weight every day, I'll perish."

"That's been my philosophy for years too," David said.

"You teach at Kent tomorrow or are you with your tutoring students?"

"Kent. Every Saturday morning. The mathematically gifted. Just like me. They're the best. I love 'em."

David watched Barry manage to fit half his first slice of pizza into his mouth all at once. David did the same.

"You're too busy," Barry mumbled through a mouthful of sausage, peppers and tomato sauce.

"It's not so bad now that dad's back in the office. Those first three months after his heart surgery were a little rough on me, to be honest."

"Yeah, you were running the show. Not doing a bad job either."

"Glad dad's back. Only there those two days this week -- taking that rehabbed heart on a little test drive -- but he'll be back in the swing of things pretty soon. You know, Barry, I hate 'running the show.'"

"I know."

"Hey, you want to go with me to create a little mischief at the Jay Townsend rally in Brooklyn Sunday?"

"You're not going to wear your hillbilly outfit again, are you?"

David had recently driven to Pennsylvania dressed in overalls and a wide-brimmed straw hat, posing as a rural newspaper reporter, to bait a Republican senate candidate into saying something racially insensitive about Obama. David could then publicize it on his blog. David had been found out before he could ask his questions, though, and had been escorted out of the rally by the candidate's staff.

"No, I'm just going straight."

"Maybe I'll go with you then. Let's see how far we get prepping tomorrow afternoon. Townsend's A-listed by the NRA. Love to throw a little disruption into his event with some of your clever questions."

"I could only do the hillbilly thing in Pennsylvania. I told 'em I was from West Virginia. Be tough to pull that off in Brooklyn, though. More napkins?"

"Yeah."

They ate in silence until each had only one slice left in his box.

"Save these til later?" Barry asked.

"Why not? I got a bag of chocolate chip cookies for us too."

"I was hoping you'd have a bunch of those little heart shaped sugar candies for us. You know, with the cute little sayings on them. Tomorrow's Valentine's Day."

"Barry, the last time I ever got a valentine was from Rosemary Feinstein in the fifth grade."

"Right," Barry could tell that was a sensitive subject. "How 'bout your court case? Any news? You haven't said anything about it in awhile."

"My dad says his friend over in the Chancellor's Office told him he expects the court's going to end this thing – one way or the other -- in the next couple of days. Maybe they're done stalling. I mean, it's only been seven years."

"Wouldn't want to rush anything, would they? Couple days, huh? You're going to be ecstatic when this thing's finally over."

"If it goes my way, I will. My dad, too. Took a lot out of him."

"But not you? C'mon."

"Hell, no. I just keep putting it back in." David lifted his pizza box and patted his stomach.

"You're the man."

"That I am."

"Let's do some torts."

"Let's. Wait a minute," David said. "What's this?" David stuck his finger into the middle of Barry's chest and when Barry looked down, David swiped his fingers up and across Barry's chin.

Barry shook his head angrily for a second, then laughed.

David loved it.

The next morning David began feeling faint during his second class of students at Kent and he went to the director's office during his break between classes.

"I'm feeling pretty woozy," David told him. "Chest hurts. I don't think I can continue on today. Sorry, John."

"You look terrible, David. Why don't you take off. I'll finish your classes for you this morning."

On his drive home all David could think about was how good a long hot shower would feel.

Mrs. Blinkoff shuffled down the hallway, grocery bag pressed up against her chest, fumbling with her apartment keys. She lived in the apartment across from David and ever since her husband had died, she had taken it upon herself to watch out for David. He was an unusual young man, she thought, but she liked him, and he always helped her carry her packages in or scrape the snow off her car windows or just kid around with her if they were doing their laundry together downstairs.

When she reached her apartment, she saw David's door was open.

"David? David?" she called in through the open doorway. No answer, but she could hear the shower running.

She set her grocery bag down against the door frame and tiptoed into the apartment.

"David?"

She moved slowly through the living room, peeking into the kitchen and then going over to the hallway to David's bedroom and the bathroom across from it. She could still hear the running water.

David's legs, naked and hairy, stretched out across the carpeted hallway from the bathroom doorway.

Mrs. Blinkoff gasped and turned back into the living room. She picked up David's phone and dialed 911.

The EMT's arrived, but they could not revive David. He had died of a heart attack. He was thirty-seven.

EPILOGUE

Three weeks after David's death, the New York Board of Education offered to settle his suit against them for harassment and retaliation. David was no longer a threat to them, and because he was dead, they could reduce the amount of the settlement they offered because they would no longer be responsible for the loss of his future income.

No known disciplinary action was taken by the school system against Menendez, Harrison or Schneider.

The following January the New York Court of Appeals, Second Circuit, ruled on his First Amendment violation suit against the New York Board of Education. In a six page response, the majority ruled against David's grievance, but in both the majority opinion and the dissenting discussion, the value of the case was noted, and applauded, for future employees in similar situations.

David lost his case, but because of it, "little guys" won.

ABOUT THE AUTHORS

Michelle Weintraub Riklan is David's older sister. Michelle and David fought often, when they were children. Usually, because David was sneaky and always successfully getting Michelle into trouble for something he did! As adults, Michelle was the surrogate matriarch and the fighting continued, often around Michelle's lack of math skills, no sense of direction, and questionable driving abilities. Michelle is the Chief Career Marketing Strategist of a boutique outplacement firm a mother to three awesome teenagers who lost the most loving and devoted Uncle they could have asked for.

Karen Weintraub is David's younger sister. Karen is a Vice President at a software company. Since David's passing 2009, Karen knew his story was meant to be told. Karen fondly remembers her time with David, especially when they were children. They played games, most notably scrabble. Karen is a self-proclaimed coffee addict who loves to sing , spend time with Dan, her dogs and relax in the Adirondacks.